Gabrielle Kent

KNIGHTS AND BIKES

REBEL BICYCLE CLUB

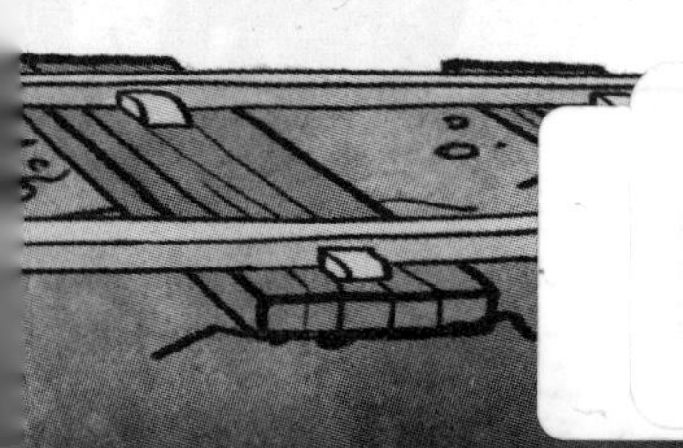

D0529845

90710 000 454 264

KNIGHTS OF
Published by Knights Of
Knights Of Ltd, Registered Offices: 119 Marylebone Road,
London, NW1 5PU

www.knightsof.media
First published 2019
001

Written by Gabrielle Kent
Text and cover copyright © Foam Sword, 2019
Illustration copyright © Foam Sword, 2019
All rights reserved
The moral right of the author and illustrator has been asserted

Set in 12pt Baskerville Regular
Design and Typeset by Marssaié Jordan
Printed and bound in the UK

All rights reserved. No part of this publication may be reproduced or transmitted in any form or by any means, electronic or mechanical, including photocopying, recording, or any information storage or retrieval system, without prior permission in writing from the publishers.
If you are reading this, thank you for buying our book.

A CIP catalogue record for this book will be available from the British Library

ISBN: PB: 978-1-9996425-4-9

2 4 6 8 10 9 7 5 3 1

LONDON BOROUGH OF
RICHMOND UPON THAMES
90710 000 454 264
Askews & Holts 08-Jan-2021
JF
RTWH
DISCARDED FROM RICHMOND UPON THAMES LIBRARY SERVICE

Gabrielle Kent

KNIGHTS AND BIKES

REBEL BICYCLE CLUB

Illustrated by Rex Crowle

and Luke Newell

Based on the Knights And Bikes video game
from Foam Sword Games!

Map of Penfurzy

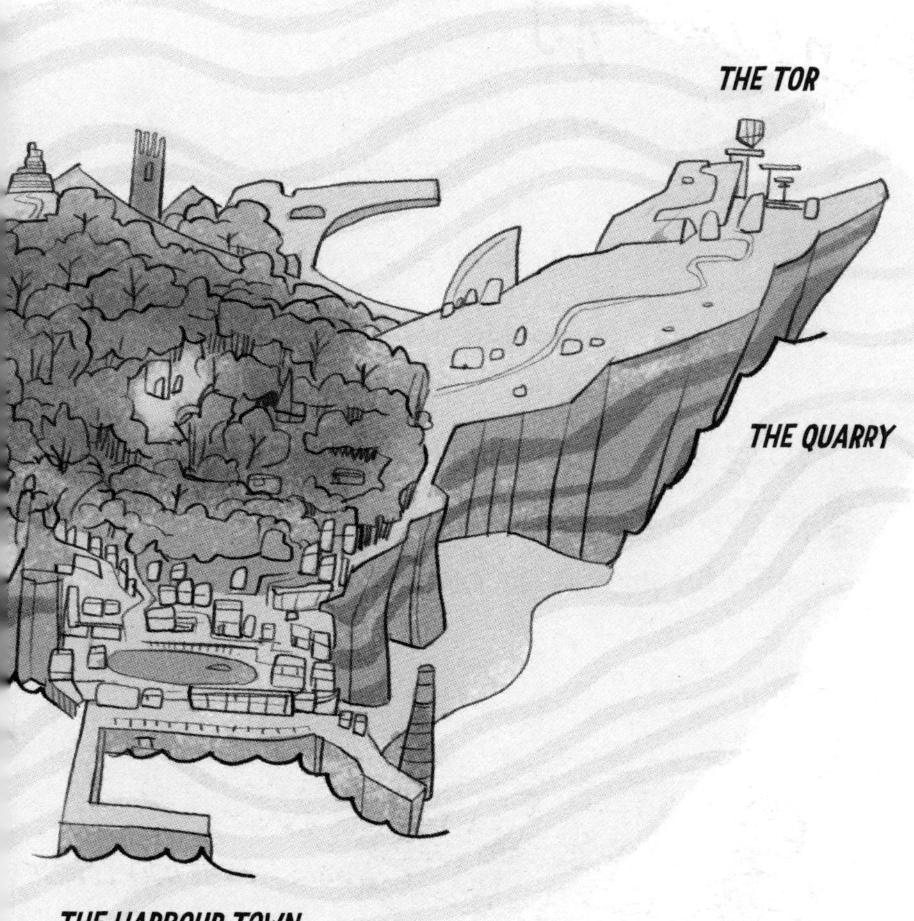
THE TOR
THE QUARRY
THE HARBOUR TOWN

ALSO BY GABRIELLE KENT

Knights & Bikes

Published By Scholastic:

Alfie Bloom and the Secrets of Hexbridge Castle

Alfie Bloom and the Witch of Demon Rock

Alfie Bloom and the Talisman Thief

THIS BOOK IS FOR YOU,

______________________,

INSERT NAME HERE

OFFICIAL MEMBER OF THE
PENFURZY REBEL BICYCLE CLUB

Chapter One

THINGS THAT GO BUMP IN THE KNIGHT

'Bang, bang, bang!' said Nessa, shining her torch under her chin so that her glowing face hovered spookily in Demelza's pitch-black caravan. Her earrings glinted in the light and her spiky black hair cast eerie shadows on the ceiling.

Demelza's frizzy red bunches bounced as she grabbed her pet goose, Captain Honkers, and squeezed him so tight that he let out a squeaky honk like a deflating set of bagpipes. Why had she suggested sharing scary stories during their pre-Halloween sleepover? Nessa was far too good at telling them.

'Bang, bang, BANG!' said Nessa again, thumping her fist on the edge of the bunk bed. Demelza shoved a handful of popcorn into her mouth to stop her teeth chattering.

'BANG, BANG, BANG!' shouted Nessa for a third time, then leant forwards, dropping her voice to a whisper.

'Wondering why her boyfriend hadn't come back from the woods, the woman opened the door of the car, and there on the roof was a man with an axe!'

'Nooo!' squeaked Demelza, pulling her sleeping bag up over her head and peering at Nessa through a tiny gap.

'And what was that in his other hand? The thing he had been banging on the roof? He held it up in the moonlight and the woman screamed as she recognized . . . HER BOYFRIEND'S SEVERED HE—'

'LA-LA-LAAA!' shouted Demelza, shoving her fingers in her ears as she scrambled out of her sleeping bag and rolled onto the floor. ***'LA-LA-LA-LA-LAAA!'*** she screamed as she ran around the caravan to stop her legs trembling. Captain Honkers flapped up to the top bunk in fright. ***'LA-LA-LAAAAAAAAAA!'***

HONK! HONK! said Captain Honkers.

'Whoa, calm down, D!' shouted Nessa. 'It's OK, it's just a story!'

'LA-LA-LA-LA-LAAAA!' Demelza shouted even louder.

Nessa leapt off the bed and grabbed Demelza around the waist, lifting her half off the ground as her legs kept running in mid-air, sending one of her bunny slippers flying across the room and into the goldfish bowl, much to the surprise of Sir Bubbles III. 'It's OK, it's made up. It's not true!' Nessa yelled over the La-La-La's.

Demelza's legs slowly stopped running. Her bare feet dropped back down onto the carpet.

'It . . . it's not?' She twisted in Nessa's arms and scanned her face for signs that she might be fibbing.

'Of course not!' said Nessa, letting go of her. 'It's just a silly story the kids at my old school used to tell.' She switched the bedside lamp on and threw Demelza's Game Gauntlet over to her. 'Sorry I scared you. Come on, howz about we play a bit of Legend of Melder before bed?'

'I wasn't really scared, you know,' said Demelza, pulling their sleeping bags down from the bunk bed to make a little nest on the floor. 'I was just tricking you into admitting you was making it up.'

'Ah, OK,' smiled Nessa, climbing into the nest beside her and picking up the other game controller. 'Nice. You totally tricked me.'

Demelza munched through a whole packet of Opal Fruits as they watched the computer loading screen. By the time the opening fanfare of the game filled the little caravan she felt much better. She put on her Game Gauntlet and bumped fists with Nessa as the words Welcome to Luxulyan Valley appeared on the screen.

BANG, BANG, BANG.

Demelza spun round and glared at Nessa. 'That's not funny!'

Nessa wasn't laughing – Nessa was staring at the ceiling. So was Captain Honkers. He flew down from the top bunk and wriggled into their nest.

BANG, BANG, BANG.

'A head! It's a head!' yelled Demelza. She shot down under the sleeping bags and felt Captain Honkers wriggle into the cotton shelter with her.

'It's not a head!' said Nessa, though Demelza was sure her voice wobbled a bit. 'It can't be a head.'

BANG, BANG, BANG.

'It's a head!' shouted Demelza, absolutely one hundred per cent, totally and utterly positively definitely sure, beyond any shadow of a doubt, that it was, undeniably, a head.

HONK! agreed Captain Honkers from between them.

'Look, I'll go out and prove that it's not a head,' said Nessa. She got up and pulled on her boots and denim jacket over her pyjamas. 'I bet it's just the TV aerial flapping in the wind.'

Demelza peeped out of her shelter. Nessa had paused with her hand on the door. She didn't look as though she wanted to open it.

'It's dangerous to go alone,' said Demelza.

Nessa gave her a relieved grin and held out her hand. 'Come on then, D.'

Demelza wriggled her hand out of the Game Gauntlet and slapped it into Nessa's. 'Take this.'

'Oh, er, right. OK,' said Nessa, looking down at the Game Gauntlet as if it wasn't quite what she had expected. She donned the gauntlet and clenched her fist.

BANG, BANG, BANG.

'Go get 'em!' shouted Demelza, trying to think of something rousing to say. 'Death or glory!'

Nessa took a deep breath, threw open the door and stepped into the night. Demelza cuddled Captain Honkers.

Honk!

'It's OK, Honkers, Nessa is super tough.'

Honk?

'All right. If she's not back in ten seconds we'll go rescue her.' She pulled him closer. 'One, two three,' she counted. A flash of light came through the window as Nessa shone her torch up at the roof. 'Four, five, six,' as Nessa's footsteps squelched around the caravan. 'Seven, eight, nine . . .'

The footsteps had stopped. Demelza lowered the sleeping bag and picked up a badminton racquet.

'Tttttt-eeeeeehhhhhhhhh-nnnnnnnnnnnnnn,' she said as slowly as she possibly could. 'OK, Honkers. Nessa is right, it can't possibly be a head. I'm going out there. Are you with me, Captain?' The goose waddled up behind her and looked out from between her knees. Demelza nodded and raised her racquet. 'Let's go!'

She jumped out of the door, then jumped out of her skin. Nessa was running screaming towards her!

'IT'SAHEAD-IT'SAHEAD-IT'SAHEAD!' Nessa yelled, leaping into the caravan and dragging Demelza with her. Captain Honkers flapped after them, sending feathers floating like snow. Nessa slammed the door and dragged furniture across it.

'What was it?' asked Demelza, grabbing Captain Honkers and shielding him from flying debris as Nessa flung everything she could in front of the door.

Nessa grabbed her by the shoulders and shook her. 'A head, D! It's a head!' she shouted, eyes wild. She dragged Demelza to the floor and flung the sleeping bags over them both.

'Are you . . . are you reaaaallly sure?' said Demelza. Something about seeing her usually cool and calm friend panicking made Demelza feel strangely brave. She gently pulled her Game Gauntlet from Nessa's hand and put it on.

'Wait, what are you doing?' asked Nessa as Demelza wriggled out from under the sleeping bags.

Demelza picked up her racquet again and pushed aside the junk in front of the door. There was no way there could be a head outside, and if she went out and proved that then she would be even braver than Nessa, and Nessa was the bravest person in the whole world.

'Seriously, don't go out there, D.'

Demelza looked her straight in the eyes and made a fist with the gauntlet. 'If I don't come back, look after Honkers for me.'

Nessa nodded as the goose hopped up onto her knee.

Honk! he said.

'Don't worry, I'll be careful,' said Demelza. She breathed deeply, then threw open the door, jumped down onto the little welcome mat and yelled into the night with a bloodcurdling

'Raaaaargh!'

THUNK!

Something fell from the roof of the caravan and splatted onto the wet ground in front of her. Demelza stopped roaring and squinted at the thing lying in the grass. She bent down for a closer look. She blinked three times, then looked again.

It was a head.

Most definitely, a head.

A severed head.

A blue-tinged, completely bodiless head.

A white-bearded, big-nosed, very dead head.

It lay in the grass staring up at her with glassy, lifeless eyes. Then it blinked. Demelza fell back and hit her bum hard on the caravan step. She had used up all of her breath in her roar and couldn't even shout for Nessa until she remembered how to breathe.

The head shuddered, wriggled and flopped up onto its severed neck. It gave her a piercing glare.

'Was all that shouting absolutely necessary?' it grumbled. Then it bounced on its neck-stump, hopping over to the welcome mat, up and over Demelza and into her caravan.

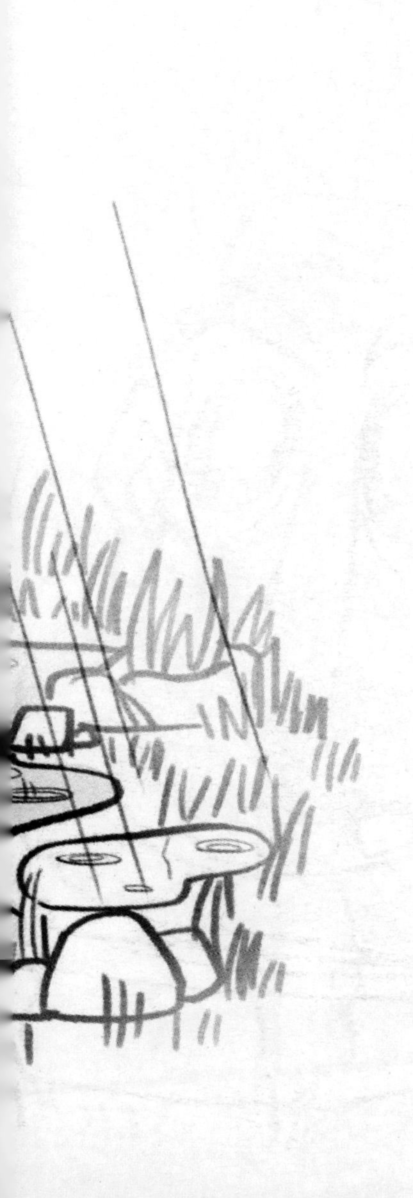

Chapter Two
THE PICKLED KNIGHT RETURNS

'AAAARRRRGH!'

Demelza scrambled up the steps as Nessa's yells poured out of the caravan. It was chaos inside. The head had clamped its jaws onto the pillow Nessa had whacked it with and was flying around in the air as she tried to shake it loose. With a great ***riiiiiiiiiiiiiip*** the pillow tore open and feathers exploded across the room as the head dropped to the floor. Captain Honkers dived towards it and began pecking at its eyes and nose.

'Call. Off. Your. Demon!' yelled the head. The voice sounded familiar. Demelza peered through the floating feathers. She had only met one talking severed head before. Could this be the same one? The head that they had met inside Penfurzy Castle during their hunt for its cursed treasure?

'It *is* you!' she said, pulling Captain Honkers away as the goose pulled out a tuft of its beard and gulped it down. 'The pickled knight. You got your head lopped off by one of the other Penfurzy knights.'

'My name,' said the pickled knight, 'is Sir Calenick.'

'Oh yeah! The pickled knight,' said Nessa, dropping the empty pillow and crouching on the feathery floor to look at the head. 'I thought your spirit was freed along with all the others when we broke the curse on the treasure you lot stole.'

The head looked a little uncomfortable. 'Ah. Well, almost. But there may have been one or two other things I, er, borrowed during my lifetime. It appears I need to return those too.'

'So, you nicked stuff other than the stuff you got cursed for nicking?' said Nessa, wafting feathers out of her face. 'I'm sooooo surprised.' Demelza didn't think she looked surprised at all. The pickled knight noticed this too.

'Yes, well, things were different in those days,' he said.

'You mean people didn't mind their stuff getting nicked?' said Nessa.

'No . . . well, yes . . . but it wasn't just me. Everyone was doing it,' said the head.

'If everyone jumped into a fire, would you?' said Demelza, copying the voice her dad used whenever he caught her doing anything super-exciting.

The pickled knight looked down towards where his feet would be, if he still had feet. 'I came here to ask for your help. I thought that if anyone could help me locate lost treasures, it would be you two, the Imp and the Trespasser. If you do not wish to join my quest, I shall take my leave.' He took a teeny-tiny hop towards the door.

Squelch.

'Away into the night.' He took another little hop.

Squelch.

'Off into the darkness.'

Squelch.

'Out of your lives.'

Squelch.

'For evermore.'

Squelch.

'Never to return.'

Squelch.

He teetered on the top step, looking back at them out of the corner of his eye.

Demelza looked at Nessa.

Nessa raised an eyebrow. 'A quest, eh?' She shrugged. 'We could get on board with that.'

Demelza clapped her hands, scaring Captain Honkers who had waddled over for another look at the pickled knight's juicy eyeballs.

'We're the best questers in Penfurzy,' she said. 'So, what are we questing for?'

'Maybe we should clean him up a bit before he tells us,' said Nessa, pinching her nose.

Demelza looked down at the muddy knight's straggly wet hair and the greeny-brown goopy puddle that was spreading on the carpet from his severed neck. 'Good idea.'

Captain Honkers watched from the safety of the top bunk as Demelza filled the sink and poured in half a bottle of her bubbliest bubble bath.

'Unhand me!' cried the pickled knight as Nessa swept him up, plunged him into the bubbles and began scrubbing with a dish brush.

'Aargle, wargle!' he spluttered as Demelza tackled his smelly brown teeth with her old toothbrush, the one she kept for cleaning her toenails.

'Keep still!' she shouted as they shampooed his yellowed hair and beard. 'The bubbles are getting up your nose.'

'Aaaargh-chooo!'

There was a loud pop. One of the knight's eyeballs rocketed across the room.

'See!' shouted Nessa triumphantly. 'I told you that's what happens when you don't close your eyes when you sneeze.'

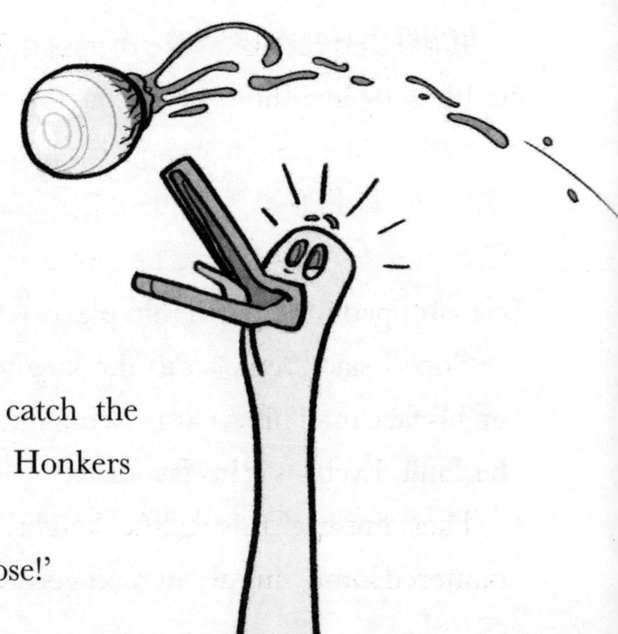

Demelza rushed to catch the eyeball before Captain Honkers could peck it up.

'Stop that goose!'

screamed the pickled knight, trying to launch himself out of the sink. 'Noooooo!' he screamed as Captain Honkers snapped up the eyeball in his beak and flapped around the caravan as Demelza tried to wrestle it from him.

'Bad Honkers! Spit! Spit it out! Now!' she shouted, prising his beak open as he tried to pop his juicy prize and guzzle the delicious jelly inside.

The pickled knight leapt out of Nessa's soapy grasp and launched himself into Demelza and Captain Honkers like a soggy cannonball.

'Oof!' said Demelza.

HONK! said Honkers. He dropped the eyeball and retreated to his bunk in a shower of flying foam.

The pickled knight scooped up the eyeball in his mouth, rolled back so that he was looking up at the ceiling, then spat it high into the air, opening his empty eye socket wide so that the eye dropped back down into place.

'Sorry,' said Demelza as the knight blinked and scrunched up his face until his eye was facing the right way again. 'It's not his fault. Eyeballs *is* his favourite.'

They finished rinsing the knight's hair and beard as he muttered something about roast goose. Both head and Honkers kept their eyes locked warily on each other as Demelza ran the hairdryer over the knight. Nessa grabbed her hair gel and combed and styled his hair and beard – now a snowy white - then powdered his face so that it didn't look quite so blue.

'Whaddya think?' said Nessa, holding up a mirror.

'What have you done to my flowing locks?' shrieked the knight as he saw the spine of hair standing up along the centre of his head.

'It's a Mohican,' said Demelza. 'You look cool.'

'Then I would rather look warm!' said the knight. 'Undo it immediately.'

'OK-OK, geez-louise!' said Nessa, combing his hair back down.

'You can leave the eyes,' he said, turning his head to admire the black ink Nessa had applied like eyeliner.

'Right, tell us about the quest!' said Demelza, excited to get started now that the knight smelled a lot better and had stopped oozing on the floor. She popped him onto a shelf so that he could talk down to them - something she remembered he enjoyed doing - then scrooched onto the bottom bunk next to Nessa. 'Right, what are we looking for, and where is it?'

'That's where I'm having a few problems,' said the head.

'After centuries bobbing around in the sea with only fish for company, my memory isn't what it used to be. The only thing that springs to mind is a chalice.'

'A chalice?' Demelza scratched her nose. 'That's like, a fancy cup?'

'Quite. This one was rather plain and made of wood rather than gold, but I remember Sir Bude saying it was rather special. It belonged to a king buried here on Penfurzy. I believe he was rather famous.'

'This cup,' said Nessa. 'I'm guessing it was buried with the king, right?' Demelza noticed the head take a sudden interest in the Slinky spring on the shelf next to him rather than meet Nessa's gaze. 'How did you get hold of it then?'

The pickled knight nudged the Slinky off the side of the shelf and ooohed and ahhhed as it climbed down two shelves before dropping to the ground. He peered at the girls to see if his distraction had worked. It hadn't.

'Well?' said Demelza.

The pickled knight sighed. 'Sir Bude, Sir Cubert and I were carousing one summer's eve and, you know how it is, one of them dared me to break into the Great Barrow.'

'What's car-OW-zzzzing?' asked Demelza. She liked the sound of the word.

'Boozing and being daft and loud,' said Nessa. 'What's the Great Barrow?'

'I know, I know!' Demelza stretched her hand up to the ceiling, then went pink as she remembered she wasn't in school and put it down very quickly. 'It's a mound of earth that people from a long-long-long-long-long-long time ago were buried inside. Mum said there's a few on Penfurzy. One got all dug up when they built that new housing estate. There was all pottery and bones an' stuff in it. Connan Lenteglos said the houses are all haunted by the people who were buried there.'

'AS I WAS SAYING . . .' hollered the pickled knight,

tired of being ignored during his own story. 'Bravely, I entered the tomb. Inside was a great throne upon which sat a sword, shield, crown and a cup. The cup didn't look particularly special, so I took it to prove I went all the way inside. Besides, I couldn't remember where I'd left my tankard and I needed something to drink mead out of.'

'What's so special about the cup then?' asked Nessa.

'I'm not sure, but I always felt wonderful after I drank out of it. It seemed to cure any illness I had. I think it might have something to do with why I survived my head being lopped off and bobbing around in the sea for centuries, even outside the magical curse on Penfurzy Castle that preserved my fellow knights.'

'So, you just have to return the cup then?' said Demelza. 'Easy-peasy, lemon-squeezy.'

'Yes, well . . .' sniffed the pickled knight. 'It would be, if I could remember where the barrow was, or what happened to the cup.'

'You don't have any idea where either of them are?' asked Nessa.

The knight leant over to scratch his forehead thoughtfully on the corner of a Rubik's Cube. 'I tattooed the location of the barrow on my arm so that I could go back and—' He stopped and glanced quickly at Nessa. 'Borrow some more stuff. The tattoo should still be on my body.'

'Nope,' said Demelza. 'They found your bones on top of the tower where your head got chopped off. The birds an' worms had eaten you all up and now your skellington is in the museum in town . . .' She paused as a look of horror passed over the knight's face. 'It's a very nice skellington,' she added quickly. 'Very clean, no maggoty bits at all.'

'Then all is lost,' moaned the knight. 'I am fated to wander this land, searching for a lost cup to return to a place that can never be found. A lonely traveller on an impossible quest. Doomed to forever roam — Mmmph!' He stopped mid-lament as Nessa slapped her hand over his mouth.

'Quit the dramarama! Of course we'll find it. You've got me, D, and Captain Honkers on your team. Quest accepted. But first,' she turned to Demelza, 'I need a new steed!'

GET A
GRIP

Chapter Three
NESSA'S NEW STEED

Boop-boop-beep-boop-beep-beeeep-booop!

'Whoa! What about this one?' whooped Demelza, pushing all of the red buttons on a futuristic-looking white bicycle until its boops and beeps filled the little bike shop. 'It has a digital speedometer. Diiiiigitaaaal! It's like a computer on wheels.'

'Meh. It just makes noises, it doesn't do anything really cool,' said Nessa. 'I want to spend the money Mum and Dad gave me on a bike I can do rad tricks on.

Noisy toys are for babies.'

'Yeah, babies,' blushed Demelza, shifting her heavy backpack on her shoulder and moving on to a different bike with chunky wheels and stunt pegs.

Nessa whistled as she looked it up and down. 'Now that is one sweet ride,' she said, climbing onto the bike, gripping the wide handlebars and bouncing up and down. 'Feels good and the black and chrome looks wicked.'

'Good choice,' said the store owner as he left the counter to join them.

'Nessa, this is Oba Sekibo,' said Demelza, tipping her head back to look aaaaall the way up at him. 'He was a champion racer before he set up this shop. He knows *everything* about bikes!'

'I built that one myself,' the man said proudly as he shook Nessa's hand. 'Just finished yesterday. There's been a lot of interest in it already. It's fast, but I built it more for stunts and off-road cycling. Those tyres will handle anything, and the seat will keep you comfy no matter how hard you land.'

'That's very important,' said Demelza, thinking of the long-padded seat on her own bike. 'Who's been looking at it, Oba?'

He nodded towards the window where a scowling boy with curly brown hair was standing, nose to the glass, watching them checking out the bike. A lanky, slightly cross-eyed dog sat by his feet, drooling onto the window sill.

'Connan Lenteglos,' Demelza hissed through her teeth. 'The most annoying, lyingest, worstest boy at school. Nessa, you have to buy this bike. It's far too cool for him to get his stink all over it!'

'What extras can I get if I buy it right now?' asked Nessa.

Oba rubbed his chin as he walked around the shop, grabbing items from the shelves and slapping them down on the counter.

'Reflectors, front and back lights, some neon beads for the spokes, a bike lock, and a puncture repair kit.'

'Ooooh!' said Demelza as Nessa looked at the haul, then picked up a yellow plastic siren with a little microphone attached.

'And this?' Nessa looked Oba straight in the eyes.

'Done,' he nodded. 'I'll attach all the kit and you can pick it up tomorrow, just in time for Halloween. One more thing . . .' He ran his hand over the plain black frame. 'I like to name all of my bikes before I sell them, but I didn't have time to paint one on this beauty. Any ideas?'

Nessa and Demelza looked at each other and smiled.

'Neon Justice TWO!' said Nessa, holding up her hand with two fingers raised in a peace symbol.

'In honour of a brave steed who left us too soon,' said Demelza, hand over her heart.

Connan was nowhere to be seen when they left the shop.

‘Probably off crying cos you’ve got the bestest bike on Penfurzy!’ said Demelza. ‘Well, after *you*,’ she whispered to her own bike, hugging it and dinging its bell as she wheeled it towards the park.

They searched through the grass for some of the year’s last conkers as they walked under the horse chestnut trees by the bandstand.

‘In my last school, I had a conker so tough it could split concrete,’ said Nessa as they sat down on the bandstand and dropped the conkers into Demelza’s backpack.

‘Desist!’ shouted the backpack.

‘Oops, sorry!’ whispered Demelza. She peeked in and saw the pickled knight’s watery blue eyes glaring up at her. ‘I forgot you was in there.’

‘Forgot I was here?’ growled the knight. ‘I trust you haven’t forgotten your promise to assist me on my quest!’

‘Of course not!’ said Demelza. ‘We was just picking a new steed for Nessa so’s we can start questing for your lost cup.’

‘The quest might not take as long if you could suggest some places for us to look,’ said Nessa.

‘Dem-elz-a, Dem-elz-a, I knew that I could smellz-ya!’ sang a voice that made Demelza’s hands and toes curl into claws.

She spun around. 'Con-nan, the . . . er . . .' Demelza spat as Connan Lenteglos laughed at her struggle to think of anything that rhymed with his name.

He threw a ball for his bandy-legged dog to chase. 'Why you talking to yer bag, Smellza?' he asked as he waggled a stick between the bandstand railings to break the spider webs glistening there.

'None of your beeswax.' Demelza hoisted the backpack onto her shoulders with only the slightest grunt from the pickled knight.

'You were talking about treasure. You hunting more treasure? Like the magic disappearing treasure you lied about finding in the castle?' A big spider made a dash for the safety of the handrail as Connan broke its web.

'We DID find treasure. Didn't we, Nessa?' said Demelza. She glared at Connan as he followed the spider along the rail, trying to get it to run onto his stick. 'Just like we're going to find the magic lost cup of the king—' She stopped as Nessa gave her a little nudge.

'What magic lost cup?' Connan sneered, as he finally caught the spider on the end of the stick.

Demelza zipped her lips closed.

'Yeah. Like I thought. Making it up,' said Connan. 'Anyway, I'm just warning you and your friend to keep your mitts off that bike you were looking at. That's mine.'

'Should have been quicker then, Con-man,' said Nessa, waving the bike shop receipt in front of him. 'I'm picking her up in the morning.'

'It's not a *her!*' wailed Connan. 'And that bike's mine, not yours!' He flicked the stick, sending the huge spider flying at Nessa's face. She caught it mid-air, placed it gently back on the railing and took a step towards wide-eyed Connan.

'General Barkley!' squeaked Connan, looking for his dog which was bounding around happily, searching for other dogs to sniff. Nessa took another step towards him. 'Baaark-leee!' he shouted again.

The dog bounced over, one ear inside out, eyes crossed as he sniffed and growled at Demelza's backpack. The bag growled back. Demelza spun around to keep it away from the dog, but he was already tugging at the canvas.

'You got that dumb goose in there?' said Connan. 'The General loves goose for dinner. He—'

He stopped as the dog let out a huge yelp and pulled his nose out of the hole he had torn in the backpack, tucked his tail between his legs and raced away across the park, tripping up Connan as he tried to grab him by the collar.

'Get back here, stupid dog. It's just a dumb goose!' shouted Connan as he gave chase. 'You'd better be lying about that bike, or you're dead meat!' he yelled over his shoulder.

'Smell you later!' Nessa yelled after him.

'Do you think he heard much?' asked Demelza.

'Nah,' said Nessa. 'He's just annoyed that I've got the raddest bike on Penfurzy.'

'SECOND raddest,' Demelza whispered to her own bike.

'So, your Pickled Knightness' - Nessa peered into the backpack - 'isn't there *anything* you remember about what happened to the cup?'

The head wriggled away from a Rubik's Cube that was poking him in the temple and sighed, 'Alas, no. But didst I hear mention of All Hallow's Eve?'

'Halloween? Yeah, it's tomorrow,' said Nessa. 'Why?'

'On that night the border between the worlds is thin and the dead walk among us. Perhaps we will meet someone who knows what happened to the cup.'

'Someone . . . dead?' asked Demelza, not even surprised. She'd lost count of the number of dead people she'd spoken to since beginning her first quest with Nessa. 'Where will we find them?'

'Wherever the most humans are gathered,' said the knight. 'The life energy of the living attracts them, like moths to flames.'

'So, I guess we need to go wherever everyone else is tomorrow night?' sighed Nessa, looking to Demelza who punched the air with excitement.

'We're going triiiiick or treeeating!' she shouted.

NEON JUSTICE II

Chapter Four

THE PENFURZY REBEL BICYCLE CLUB

Nessa wheelied up to Demelza's house early the next morning on her sparkling new bike which bore the words NEON JUSTICE II in green neon paint along the jet-black frame. Demelza shielded her eyes as the sun glanced off the perfect chrome, and promised herself she'd chip some of the mud off her own bike to see if the mudguards were still shiny under there.

After a breakfast of Yarg and crackers, the day was spent in Demelza's caravan preparing Halloween costumes and packing supplies for their quest. Into backpacks went torches, dice, a pack of playing cards, water-balloons, bubbles, a whistle, rubber gloves, a penknife, drawing pins, a ruler, a plunger, a packet of felt tips, a first aid kit, pickled onion crisps and a bottle of cherryade.

'What hast thou there?' asked the pickled knight as Demelza grabbed a packet of bangers from a drawer. She took out one of the little twists of white paper and threw it out of the door where it exploded on the caravan steps with a sharp BANG!

'They've got gunpowder and grit inside them,' she explained.

'And what be they for?' asked the knight.

'Duh! For going BANG!' said Demelza.

'Whaddya think, D?' said Nessa, pulling on the cardboard breastplate and helmet she had just finished painting.

'Awesome!' Demelza ran her hand over the silver-painted dragon emblem on the breastplate. 'Give me a hand with mine.'

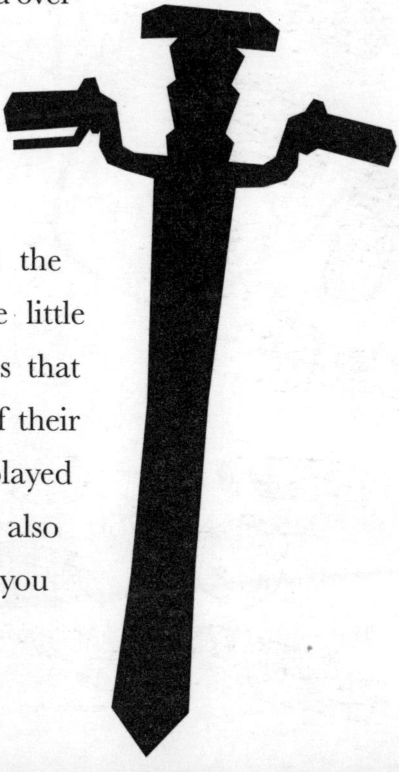

As the sun dropped lower in the autumn sky, two knights left the little caravan. They attached the poles that held their banners onto the backs of their wheeled steeds. Each banner displayed the image of a sword, which could also be a bike wheel and handlebars if you looked at it the right way.

'Cool banners,' said Demelza's dad as he hurried over with his camera.

'It's the logo of our gang, the Penfurzy Rebel Bicycle Club,' interrupted Demelza before her dad – who had once been a roadie for a rock band - started telling embarrassing stories about his old band, Pontefract. 'Nessa made up the name and I designed the logo.' She spat on her hand and high fived Nessa, then they fist bumped, tickled elbows, bumped hips and punched their right fists high in the air. 'That's our official handshake.'

'Unhygienic, but not bad,' said Demelza's dad. He wound on the film in his camera. 'Right then, say cheeeeese!'

'YAAAAARG!' shouted Demelza and Nessa, holding their swords aloft.

'One more!'

'Get in here, Sir Honk-a-lot,' called Demelza as her dad wound on the film again. Captain Honkers waddled between the bikes and spread his wings wide. He honked loudly through his tiny cardboard helmet as the bright flash lit up the whole caravan park. They posed for several more pictures with their shields, foam swords and cardboard lances while the pickled knight played completely dead in the basket Nessa had fixed to the front of her bike.

That's enough now, Dad,' said Demelza. 'There won't be any sweets left by the time we get to town.'

'OK. Have a good time. Just one question.' He pointed at the pickled knight who was letting his tongue loll out and had rolled his eyes back in his head so that only the whites were visible. 'What's with the mouldy old melon? I'm not sure it matches your costumes.'

'Oh, this?' Nessa pulled the knight's head out of the basket by his hair and held him up. '*This* is a severed head! We made it to warn everyone what we do to our enemies!'

'Ah, very good. Very, er, realistic,' said Demelza's dad, flinching away. 'Off you go then. Have a good time.'

He waved as they cycled out of the caravan park and down the hill towards town. Demelza wore her anorak fastened like a cape over her armour, with the hood up under her helmet. The cape fluttered behind her as they freewheeled down the hill. Captain Honkers' own tiny cape flapped as he sat proudly between her handlebars, beak turned into the wind as they sailed into town. The streets on the way were already starting to fill with ghosts, goblins, Frankenstein's monsters, Draculas and witches, all carrying carved pumpkins or turnips with little candles inside.

They knocked on the doors of people who Demelza knew and soon their pillowcase candy-bag looked like a dentist's worst nightmare. Demelza's jaw was aching from all the sweets they had eaten before they even reached the centre of town,

'Urgh, toffee!' Nessa stopped and leant her bike against a wall so that she could pick the brown sweets out of the bag and shove them into Demelza's pockets. 'Why do old people always give toffee?'

'Offing ong iff offee!' said Demelza through sticky teeth.

'What is the point of this tomfoolery?' the pickled knight demanded from Nessa's basket, causing a small ghost who had stopped to count his sweets in front of them to shriek with fright and run after his friends.

'To get sweets, of course!' said Demelza.

'Hmmph!' grunted the knight. 'You modern folk have corrupted Samhain! At the start of the dark half of the year we celebrated with fire and drink and honoured the dead, for they are closer to us on this day—'

'Whoa!' interrupted Demelza as they rounded the corner to an incredible sight.

The town centre was thronged with actual, real ghosts!

Transparent shimmering ghosts, Victorian ghosts, medieval ghosts, ancient ghosts, ghosts in flares and flowery shirts, all were drifting around alongside humans who didn't even notice they were there.

'Why can we see them and no one else can?' asked Nessa, spinning to watch a ghost drift past on a transparent Harley-Davidson.

'Because I anointed your eyes while you were sleeping,' said the pickled knight.

'What with?' asked Nessa.

'My saliva,' said the pickled knight. 'It has given you the ability to see the dead.'

Nessa's eye's narrowed. 'You're telling me you licked our eyelids?'

The pickled knight winced. 'Urgh, lick your eyelids indeed! Of course not! I spat on them from my shelf.'

Demelza paused halfway through picking her nose to waggle her finger at the pickled knight. 'That . . . is disgusting!'

'Aha! The Dread Witch of Bullion Cove!' said Sir Calenick, flinching away from the finger and nodding towards a transparent woman in a long dress. 'She's been around longer than me. If anyone knows where the cup went, it's her!'

Demelza had never seen a ghost witch before. But she was a bit disappointed that this witch didn't have a pointy chin, or a single wart. She looked a bit like the town librarian, Elizabeth Mawgan-Porth. She was hovering behind a young man who kept sliding along a bus stop bench to get closer to a woman sitting there. The woman kept sliding away and ignoring him as she listened to her Walkman.

As the man reached out to remove the woman's headphones, the witch waved her hands. The man gripped his stomach, leapt to his feet and ran for the public toilets as if his life depended on getting there as soon as possible.

'Hoy there, Witch!' shouted the pickled knight.

The ghost's gleeful smile turned to a look of fear, then an eyeroll as she spotted the pickled knight.

'My name, as you know perfectly well, is Demelza,' said the woman, glaring at the pickled knight as Demelza and Nessa cycled over.

'Oooh! Mine too!' gasped Demelza. 'And this is my best friend, Nessa. We're looking for—'

'An old cup,' said the pickled knight. 'Naught special - it had, um, sentimental value.'

The witch put her hands on her hips as she stared down at him. 'Just as it had sentimental value to him in the Great Barrow? Him whose tomb you took it from?'

'Oh, ha-ha. You heard tell of that?' said the pickled knight, wriggling down a bit further in the basket.

'Did you see the truth in your cauldron?' asked Demelza.

'Or did your familiar tell you?' asked Nessa.

'No,' sighed Demelza the witch. 'He bragged about it himself when he was carousing too merrily with those metal-clad moron friends of his.'

'How dare you refer to the great Penfurzy knights in such a manner,' growled the pickled knight. 'Why, we should—'

'We should thank you for sharing any information you might have about where it went,' said Nessa, tucking the knight under her arm and tapping him on the nose as if he was a bad dog.

The witch smiled at them. 'In the spirit of Samhain, I'm happy to help the *living,*' she said with a pointed stare at the pickled knight. 'The knight Calenick wasn't the only one who talked too much when merry. The vagabond, Margh, rarely joins us at Samhain, but when he does, one of his favourite stories is of the time he robbed Calenick of his money pouch, his sword, and his favourite drinking cup. Fortunately, he didn't know the importance of the cup and I believe it soon passed out of his hands.'

'Mad Margh!' shouted the pickled knight. 'I remember now! I had a drink with him after he was expelled from the Penfurzy knights. When I woke up in a field the next day everything was gone, right down to my best boots! Tell me, Dread Witch, have you seen him tonight?'

'Shhhhh!' said Nessa, clamping her hand over his mouth as a couple of little aliens wandered past with their sweet buckets.

'Again, it's just Demelza,' said the witch. 'And no, I haven't seen him tonight. He haunts the cave at the bottom of the tor - you'll probably find him there. Now, if you'll excuse me, my old coven and I are having a get-together. Nice to meet you, Demelza, Nessa,' she called over her shoulder as she drifted off to join a group of transparent women standing around the oak on the town green.

'Brilliant,' said Demelza. 'It's Saturday tomorrow, so we can cycle to the tor and take my tent in case we need to camp out while we look for the cup.'

'Rad,' said Nessa. 'My first camping trip on Penfurzy. This is going to be fun!'

'Fun?' snapped the pickled knight. 'I hope you're treating this quest with the seriousness it deserves. My afterlife depends on it!'

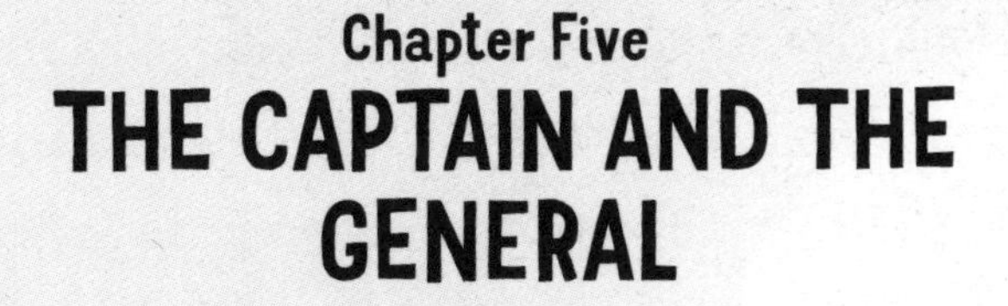

Chapter Five
THE CAPTAIN AND THE GENERAL

'Now that we know where we're going to look for the cup, how's about we go back to your caravan and play some games?' said Nessa. 'Mum and Dad said I could stay at yours again and they just bought me' - she pulled out a plastic game cartridge and waggled it in front of Demelza - 'tadaah! *Goon Gumpas II!*'

'OK, but just two more houses, or three, or six,' pleaded Demelza, shaking her bag of sugary goodies.

HONK!

'Uh-oh,' said Demelza as she spotted what Captain Honkers was honking at. Connan Lenteglos and his school friends, Jory and Trevik, were blocking the pavement further ahead. They were dressed in skeleton costumes and demanding a toll of sweets from any kid who wanted to get past. Connan was sitting on his battered BMX, General Barkley by his feet drooling out of one side of his mouth as he scratched his ear with his back leg.

'Let's go, before they see us,' said Demelza. She got onto her bike and turned towards the park, but it was too late—

General Barkley yipped excitedly as he saw Captain Honkers.

'Oi! Smellza! Your mate is riding MY bike!' shouted Connan.

'Just cos you drooled on it doesn't make it yours,' Nessa called over her shoulder as she followed Demelza towards the park. 'I bought it fair and square.'

'You *knew* I was going to buy it!' he shouted.

'Dibs doesn't work in shops, bro!' Nessa called back.

'You don't even know how to ride a bike like that,' yelled Connan. He kicked a stone after them. There was a loud DING as it bounced off Nessa's chrome mudguard.

'Uh-oh.' Demelza closed her eyes. 'Shouldn't have done that.'

Nessa pulled up into a wheelie and spun her rearing steed to face Connan and friends.

'Dude,' she growled as the front wheel bounced down onto the tarmac, almost sending the pickled knight, who was back to playing dead, flying out of her basket, 'you did NOT just mess with Neon Justice!'

'It's not Neon Justice! It's the Speed King!' said Connan.

Nessa sniggered.

'What? It's a cool name!' shouted Connan, looking back at Jory and Trevik. They shrugged.

Connan rode towards Nessa and stopped with his muddy front tyre also touching hers.

'I challenge you to a stunt contest!' he said. 'My bike for yours.'

'Ooooh!' said Demelza, Jory and Trevik.

Honk! said Captain Honkers.

'Phht! Why would I bother? I have the bike,' said Nessa.

'Oh, you're scared I'll beat you?' said Connan. 'Told you! You don't deserve the Speed King.'

Nessa clapped her hands to her face. 'Oh no, you said I'm scared. Now I guess I HAVE to do it.'

'Go on, Nessa!' said Demelza. 'You'll beat him anyway.'

Connan, Jory and Trevik burst out laughing at that.

Nessa's mouth became a hard, thin line. She gripped her handlebars, knuckles white. 'Not that I have anything to prove, but let's do this!'

Connan smiled. 'OK, this is how it works. I do a trick first. If you can't do it, I get your bike.'

'Sounds one-sided,' said Nessa, sitting back in her saddle and folding her arms. 'But sure, go for it.'

Connan tied the General to a park bench, then spat on his hands, rubbed them together and twisted his bike's handgrips as though he was revving a motorbike. He cycled over to a low wooden bar that ran around the patch of grass in the square. He hopped up onto it, landing in a wheelie which he held as he rode to the other end where he did a little jump off the end. Then he rode back to whoops from Jory and Trevik. They high fived him before turning to grin at Nessa.

Nessa yawned, rolled up her denim sleeves and rode towards the rail, easily hopping onto it in a wheelie. Demelza applauded as Nessa whizzed to the other end then leapt off the rail to bounce off a bin. Demelza whooped as Nessa spun the bike in the air to land back on the rail and cycle back to the start, all without disturbing the pickled knight from her basket.

'Wooo!' cried Demelza, heart glowing with pride as she slapped Nessa's hand in the highest of fives. The three boys tried their hardest not to look impressed.

'That's not exactly what I did,' sulked Connan.

'No, it was a bajillion times better,' said Demelza, lifting Nessa's arm high in the air. 'Nessa wins!'

'Now I'M going to choose a trick,' said Nessa. 'If you can do it, I'll give you Neon Justice, but if you can't, you shut up about my bike for ever. Deal?'

Connan looked from Jory to Trevik, unable to back out in front of his fellow skeletons. 'Deal.'

Nessa looked around the town square, then smiled as she spotted a line of round wooden posts with a chain linking each of them. She hopped up so that Neon Justice's back tyre sat on the first post, and the front tyre on the next one. In one quick move, she flipped the back end of the bike round so that the back tyre landed now on the third post, then lifted the handlebars and spun again to land the front tyre on the fourth post. Picking up speed, she spun the bike all the way along the row of posts, then bounced down to the ground on her back tyre. Staying in a wheelie, she bounced left and right over the chains all the way back to the boys, where she dropped onto her front tyre, spun the back of the bike one hundred and eighty degrees, then sat back in her saddle and folded her arms.

Jory and Trevik nodded to each other and shoved their hands in their pockets to keep from applauding as everyone turned to Connan. He gulped. With no way out he rode over to the posts.

He managed to hop his bike up onto the first two and grinned over at them, but the second he tried to flip the back end of bike around he spun straight off into a heap on the grass.

'Nessa wins!' shouted Demelza, holding her friend's hand high. Captain Honkers bounced up and down between Demelza's handlebars, honking his congratulations.

'You only won cos you used a better bike!' yelled Connan, flinging his bike aside, the chain dangling loose.

HONK! Captain Honkers flapped his wings angrily as Connan waved his finger at them.

'No, she won cos she's better than you,' shouted Demelza. 'Just admit it!'

'Never!' wailed Connan. General Barkley whined and strained at his leash and Connan stomped over to untie him.

'Smell ya later, Lenteg-lost,' Nessa waved as they turned and cycled towards the park.

Wooof! Awooof! Excited by all of the commotion, General Barkley broke free from Connan's grip and chased them through the park gates.

'Fly like the wind!' Demelza yelled as the slavering dog snapped at their ankles.

'Barkley, get back here!' yelled Connan.

Demelza and Nessa's feet were a blur as they cycled furiously. Captain Honkers shook off his helmet and launched himself from Demelza's handlebars to fly overhead, dive-bombing General Barkley and snapping at his nose, which only made the dog chase them faster.

'Come on, Honkers! Leave him!' yelled Demelza, but the goose was on a mission to slow General Barkley down so that they could get away. She looked back over her shoulder as the goose swept down for another attack, then she froze. The universe entered slow motion as the dog's jaws clamped onto the goose's wing. An ear-splitting **HONK!** filled the air.

'GET OFF HIM!' she roared, tyres and brakes squealing as she spun on the spot and rode at General Barkley. The dog was shaking Captain Honkers by the wing like a rag doll. Feathers were flying. Connan was racing towards them, his distant voice yelling at the dog to stop, but he was too far away.

HONK! HOOONK! squealed the goose.

Demelza threw down her bike, grabbed the dog by the collar and pulled, only then realizing what a terrible idea that was.

'Watch out, D!' shouted Nessa, cycling towards them. The dog let go of Honkers and turned to snap excitedly at Demelza's sleeve, barking as though this was the best game in the world.

'Let. Go. Of. *MY* imp!' roared the pickled knight as Neon Justice squealed to a halt. Nessa pulled him from her basket, swung back her arm and hurled him towards the dog. Demelza watched the head sail through the air to land with the knight's teeth clamped firmly onto General Barkley's tail.

AROOOOOOO! yelped the dog, running in circles to try and shake off the pickled knight. ***AROOOOOOOOO!***

'What did you do to my dog?' cried Connan. The pickled knight dropped to the ground and played dead again as Connan finally reached them and General Barkley jumped up into his arms. 'Scaring him with that rubbishy rubber head!'

Demelza ignored him as she scooped the shuddering Captain Honkers up into her arms. His right wing was bent in a very unnatural way. Spots of blood ran down the white feathers and onto Demelza's clothes. She tore off her cardboard armour and zipped up her anorak around the goose so that only his head poked out under her chin.

Connan and Nessa watched her in silence.

'Oh. I'm . . . I'm sorry, Demelza,' said Connan, using her name properly for the first time in his life as he saw the damage his dog had done. 'He just got over-excited.'

Demelza stared him right in the eyes as she climbed back onto her bike while Nessa grabbed the pickled knight. Her eyes were burning with tears. She imagined firing lasers out of her eyeballs and straight through Connan and his stupid, stupid dog.

'You'll pay for this, Connan Lenteglos,' she said over her shoulder as she turned her steed homewards. 'You. Will. Pay.'

Chapter Six
GONE QUESTING

Demelza buried her face in Nessa's jacket, sniffing hard to stop her nose running onto the denim as the vet tended to Captain Honkers on the kitchen table.

'That kid shouldn't be allowed a dog if he can't control it!' said Demelza's dad as he watched the vet setting the quivering goose's broken wing.

'Believe me, I'll be having words with Connan's parents about this,' said the vet as she gave Captain Honkers an injection.

'Is he . . . is he going to be OK?' Nessa asked as she handed Demelza a large checked handkerchief.

The vet glanced at Demelza's dad, then said gently, 'It's difficult to tell with birds. Even if the attack isn't too bad, the shock can be worse than the injury. I'm afraid we'll have to wait until tomorrow to see if he's out of the woods. But I promise you, I'll do everything I can to save him.'

Demelza let out a wail. Her whole world crumbled around her at the thought of losing Captain Honkers, and it was as if she was listening from underwater as the vet talked to her dad using lots of big words. It wasn't until she was back in the caravan with Nessa, sitting under sleeping bags and sipping from mugs of hot chocolate and marshmallows, that she could breathe properly again.

'I wish there was something we could do, other than just waiting,' she said, gazing out of the window towards the house where the vet and her dad were tending to Captain Honkers.

Nessa twiddled one of her earrings. 'Maybe there is,' she said slowly. 'Pickles, that cup, you said it made you feel better when you were ill. Is that true?'

'I *never* lie!' said the pickled knight. Nessa gave him a hard stare. 'OK, that was quite clearly a lie, but yes, the cup gave me a new lease of life when I feared the Black Death had me in its clutches.'

Demelza sniffed and rubbed her nose on her sleeve. 'The cup could heal Honkers?'

'I can only speak of my own experience, but if it can heal a human, I don't see why it wouldn't work on a lesser creature . . . er, I mean a fine bird like Sir Honk-a-lot!' he corrected himself as Demelza lobbed a Rubik's Cube at him.

'But it's too late, we'd need it tonight!' She threw herself back on the bed and stared up at the Care Bear stickers on the slats of the bunk above.

'Well, we're already packed,' said Nessa. She pulled out their backpacks and hoisted them onto the bed. 'We could start our quest right now. What do you think, D?' She held out her hand.

Demelza stared up at her. Was it possible? Could they find the cup that night and get back in time to save Captain Honkers?

She grasped Nessa's forearm and pulled herself up, wiping her eyes on her Game Gauntlet as she shouldered her backpack. 'Let's go!'

She scrawled a note and left it on her pillow in case her dad came out to the caravan:

All was silent as they wheeled their bikes through the cool autumn night, weaving between the caravans perched on the clifftops. Demelza looked up at the house as they crept past. The lamp was still on in the kitchen - her dad was keeping his promise of watching over Captain Honkers all night.

'Hold on, Captain,' whispered Demelza. 'We'll be back soon.' She felt Nessa squeeze her shoulder. Captain Honkers needed them. They WOULD succeed.

The full moon cast long shadows across the crazy golf course as they walked past the wonky wooden Penfurzy knights and through the shadow of Penfurzy Castle, which overlooked the golf course.

'Did I ever thank you for saving me from my watery tomb?' asked the pickled knight from Nessa's basket as the girls mounted their steeds.

'Nope,' said Nessa.

'Oh,' said the pickled knight. 'I really must remember to.'

The girls travelled in silence for a while as they followed the cliffs, then freewheeled down the grassy hill and into the woods, bike tyres crunching over a carpet of moss and orange-coloured leaves. It was dark under the canopy of branches even though most of the leaves had fallen.

It was very dark. Their bike lights and head torches cut through the gloom, casting long shadows that Demelza, in the corner of her eye, was sure were moving.

Even the pickled knight had a head torch of his own strapped to his forehead which he seemed rather impressed by as he bounced up and down in Nessa's basket shouting:

'Onward!' and 'Follow me to glory!' and 'We ride for ever!'

All good battle cries, Demelza had to admit, and they certainly made their journey through the woods less frightening. She checked the compass that she had stuck to her handlebars. They were still heading in the right direction but she had a feeling she had forgotten something important . . .

There was a hazy mist hanging low around their wheels, and suddenly a terrible sucking squelch filled the air, followed by a loud yell. She turned to see Nessa struggling to cycle as her front wheel sank into the ground. The pickled knight had flown out of her basket and caught in a bush.

'Eargh!' shouted Nessa. 'D! What's happening?'

'The marsh! I forgot about the marsh!' shouted Demelza. 'It looks so *different* in the dark. Don't move!'

'Couldn't if I wanted to!' said Nessa, pulling back on the handlebars of the bike as the front wheel disappeared and her feet and pedals began to sink.

'Hang on!' Demelza looked around frantically, then grabbed every large stick and branch she could find and flung them onto the soft ground between her and Nessa. 'The rope in your backpack,' she shouted. 'Tie it to your handlebars and throw me the other end!' Nessa scrabbled in her bag for the rope as Demelza threw more long sticks onto what was starting to look like a very untidy raft.

'Catch!' shouted Nessa, uncoiling the rope and throwing it like a lasso towards Demelza.

Demelza grabbed the end of the rope and tied it to a tree. 'Quick, flop onto the raft then wriggle to me on your stomach!' She lay down on the solid ground and held her hands out towards Nessa.

'You sure about this, D?' said Nessa, struggling to pull her feet from the slurping, squelching ground as the bike sunk deeper and deeper.

'Nope!' said Demelza. 'But it's worth a try.'

'Next time, just say yes!' said Nessa. 'Geronimo!' She threw herself off Neon Justice II and belly flopped onto the raft with a cracking of twigs and a loud squelch. It sunk slightly under her but the branches helped to spread her weight evenly across the greedy ground.

'Now crawl. On your stomach, like a commando!' shouted Demelza.

'Yes, ma'am!' said Nessa, saluting. The branches creaked and cracked as she wriggled forwards on her stomach, using her elbows to push herself forwards. 'Did I ever tell you I used to be a commando with the—'

'Not the right time!' said Demelza, before Nessa could begin one of her fantastical stories. 'Come on, just a little more . . .'

There was a loud **squaaaart** as the mud slowly devoured the raft, threatening to suck Nessa down to the centre of the earth. Demelza threw herself forwards to grab Nessa's wrists as the raft tipped backwards.

'Got you!' she yelled. 'Jump!'

Nessa scrabbled to her feet and leapt. She landed panting next to Demelza. The marsh slurped the branches down, as though searching for the juicy morsel that had sprung from its jaws.

'That . . . was close,' said Demelza.

'Noooo! Neon Justice!' shouted Nessa as the bike's front light disappeared into the mud.

'It's OK, I've got her!' Demelza untied the rope from the tree and looped it around the trunk. 'Give me a hand!'

Nessa grabbed the rope and they pulled with all their might. The marsh didn't want to give up another meal but finally, inch by inch, the light and then the wheels emerged from the muddy slop.

'Heave! HEAVE!' they yelled together as Neon Justice finally broke free of the hungry ground and slid towards them.

'It's OK. I got you!' said Nessa as she pulled the bike to safety and hugged it close. 'Thanks, D. You saved her!'

'And *who* is going to save *me*?' shouted the pickled knight.

Demelza chewed her fingers, wondering if there was any way they could save him from his wobbly perch in the bush without sinking themselves.

'It's OK. I got this,' said Nessa. She untied a bamboo pole with a green fishing net on the end that she had tied to the frame of Neon Justice. 'And you said we wouldn't need this,' she grinned. 'OK, Pickles, we're going to need you to jump,' she shouted.

Demelza grabbed the pole with her and they held it out as far as they could so that the net was less than a metre from the pickled knight. He looked at the net, then at the muddy bubbles below.

'Quickly!' said Demelza. 'It's the only way. Jump!'

'Jump, jump, jump!' chanted Nessa.

Demelza joined in. 'Jump, jump, JUMP!'

The pickled knight wriggled around until he was upright, flexed the stump of his severed neck, and with an almighty yell he launched himself from the bush. Demelza and Nessa swept the net up to catch him. The bamboo bent almost in two with the weight of the head, then flexed back so fast it sent the knight soaring waaaay up into the air.

Nessa dropped the pole and ran, looking up and back, arms ready to catch the head like a rugby ball as it dropped down towards her, the light of his head torch looming like a motorbike headlamp as he plummeted out of the sky.

'Yeeeeeaaargh!'

'Got you!' said Nessa as he cannonballed into her arms, knocking them both to the ground.

'That was brilliant!' said Demelza, taking the head from Nessa and helping her up.

'No. *That* was very undignified!' scowled the pickled knight as Demelza popped him back into Neon Justice's basket.

They picked up their bikes and wheeled them onwards, and this time Demelza was sure to take a route well away from the edge of the marsh - they couldn't save Captain Honkers if they were stuck at the bottom of a swamp.

'The train tracks!' said Demelza, as they cleared the trees to see moonlight glinting off overgrown rails. 'Brilliant! They'll take us most of the way if we follow them.'

'I didn't know any trains ran on Penfurzy?' said Nessa, hopping her bike up onto one of the iron rails and cycling along it with perfect balance.

'They don't,' said Demelza, copying Nessa's lead and wobbling down the other rail. 'Well, not passenger trains. These tracks run from the quarry to the docks, but they're not used now. Not by real trains anyway. If you believe Connan Lenteglos' - she paused to spit after she said his name - 'there's a ghost train that runs down here, but only at Halloween.'

'Soooo, tonight?' said Nessa as something toot-tooted far in the distance.

Chapter Seven
ALL ABOARD!

Demelza cocked her head to one side as she listened to the night.

'Just an owl,' she said at last.

'You're sure?' asked Nessa.

'Pretty sure. Anyways, the train tracks are the easiest route at night. We can't get lost, not when Honkers needs us!'

'OK. Besides, I suppose we have our own ghost for protection.' Nessa patted the pickled knight on the top of his head then pulled her hand away as he snapped at her fingers.

'I am *not* a ghost!' he snarled. 'Ghosts are spirits with no physical presence. I am a reanimated corporeal being!'

'Ummmm, is that like a zombie?' asked Demelza as they followed the tracks onto a red-brick viaduct.

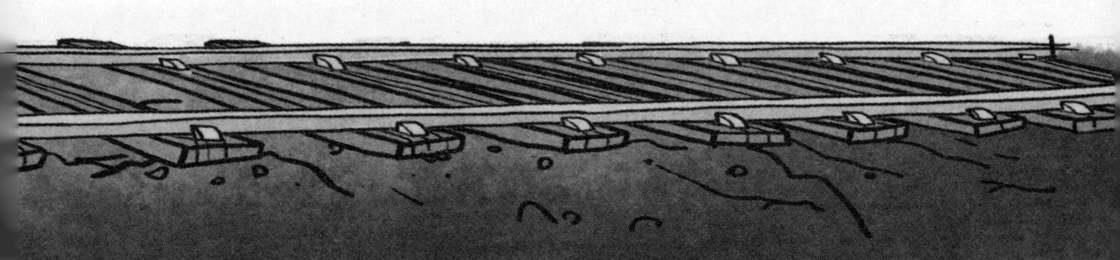

'What is a zombie?' asked the pickled knight, scowling as though unsure whether to feel insulted.

'Someone dead but still moving around,' said Nessa.

'Well, perhaps. I guess I could be . . .'

'They've got all rotten bits and if they grab you they eat your guts and brains and turn you into a zombie too,' said Demelza helpfully.

'Urgh, blurgh, then no! I am most definitely NOT a zombie,' spat the pickled knight.

'Good to know,' said Nessa.

'SHHHHH!' Demelza stopped in the middle of the viaduct and cupped her hand behind her ear to listen to a very distant noise that was getting louder by the second - ***CLICKETY-CLACK, CLICKETY-CLACK***, then a faint ***toot-toooot.***

'I thought you said this track isn't in use?' said Nessa.

'It isn't!' Demelza put her hand on the rails. There was no vibration – it couldn't be a train. Unless . . . She looked at Nessa. Nessa looked at her.

'GHOST TRAIN!' they screamed.

'Leggit!' Demelza spun her bike and began cycling back across the viaduct. It was a few seconds before she realized Nessa wasn't following. She looked over her shoulder.

Nessa was cycling in the opposite direction.

'This way!' Demelza yelled. The **CLICKETY-CLACK, CLICKETY-CLACK** grew louder and louder.

'We're closer to this side. Come on, we can make it!' Nessa shouted back.

'No! It's this way!' Demelza roared. 'Come back, Nessa!'

'Will one of you please make a decision!' shouted the pickled knight from Nessa's basket.

An eerie green glow flashed between the dark trees on the other side of the bridge as the train came closer . . .

CLICKETY-CLACK, CLICKETY-CLACK, CLICKETY-CLACK.

Nessa wheeled her bike round and cycled back towards Demelza. The pickled knight shouted for her to go faster as the glow lit the sky . . .

CLICKETY-CLACK, CLICKETY-CLACK, CLICKETY-CLACK.

Demelza looked over the wall at the side of the bridge and shivered. They were way too high above the valley to jump.

'Come on, Nessa!'

Nessa reached her and they pedalled as fast as they could at opposite sides of the track. The glow of the train was so bright it cast their shadows, long and thin, in front of them. As she tried to glance over her shoulder Demelza's tyre hit a lump of rock, sending her flying over her handlebars to land headfirst in a patch of weeds at the side of the track.

'Demelza!' There was a clatter as Nessa dropped Neon Justice to pull Demelza to her feet. But it was too late.

CLICKETY-CLACK,
CLICKETY-CLACK,
CLICKETY-CLACK.

Demelza leant against Nessa, shielding her eyes from the blinding glow.

'We stand together!' shouted the pickled knight, rolling out of the basket and bouncing squelchily over to join them.

Demelza blinked against the light and stared at the monstrous train hurtling towards them. There was nowhere to run.

TOOT! TOOOOOOOOOT!

Green smoke poured from the funnel of the glowing green demonic steam train. A ghost driver in a flat cap leant out of the cabin, staring straight ahead as the train loomed over them.

CLICKETY-CLACK,
CLICKETY-CLACK,
CLICKETY-CLACK.

TOOT!

8001

TOOOOOOOOOT!

Demelza and Nessa grabbed each other. The pickled knight jumped up into their arms.

'So long, Nessa!' said Demelza.

'Later, D.'

'Farewell, brave sisters!' shouted the pickled knight as they all closed their eyes.

Demelza thought being hit by a train would be a very quick way to die. She hadn't expected it to *tickle.* She opened her eyes. The train had gone straight through them! In fact, it was still going through them. Ghostly green wagons full of rocks whizzed past as the train steamed onwards.

'Yuk! It feels like someone has put their hand through my stomach and is playing around in my guts,' said Nessa.

'THIEF!' shouted the pickled knight so loudly Demelza nearly dropped him.

A ghost was zooming towards them atop a wagon filled with rocks. He was wearing what looked like a sack tied at the waist with rope and his beard hung down to his overgrown toenails. His long hair whirled around him as he whooped and danced on top of the rocks.

'Mad Margh!' yelled the pickled knight as the strange figure whizzed past them.

The ghost paused his mad dance and stared down in surprise.

'Get back here, Margh, you varlet!' the pickled knight screamed in rage. He leapt out of their arms and bounced after the train on his neck stump.

The ghost grinned and jumped down from the wagon as the train disappeared into the night.

'Ooh, he's done it now,' said Demelza.

The ghost threw his transparent beard over his shoulder and strode towards them, feet disappearing slightly into the ground with each step until he stood over the pickled knight, who glared up at him, unflinching.

'Not sure I like the look of him,' said Nessa, nudging Demelza's arm. 'Maybe we should get out of here?'

'The train went right through us,' said Demelza. 'Perhaps he can't actually hurt us either?'

'Calenick! It IS you!' The ghost put his hands on his hips as he bent down to inspect the pickled knight.

'Bit shorter than when I last saw ye!'

'That's SIR Calenick, weasel!' shouted the pickled knight, bouncing up and down as though trying to head-butt the ghost.

'Still got that temper though,' giggled the ghost.

'Where is it?' yelled the pickled knight. 'I know you took my cup. I remember now. We were carousing after the Great Tournament and when I woke up my money, sword, cup and best boots were gone. Why, I should—'

'What? Bite my ankles?' laughed the ghost, dancing gleefully around the head. 'Come on then, Calenick. Have a go. You were always too slow for me.'

'Stop that!' growled the pickled knight as the ghost leapt over him. 'I can see right up your tunic.'

'Shouldn't be lookin' then,' said the ghost. 'Now, if ye don't mind, I'll be off. You made me miss my lift into town, on party night too!' The ghost began to skip away after the train.

'Wait!' Nessa called after him. 'What happened to the cup?'

The ghost paused and looked over his shoulder. 'Why? Was there something special about it?'

'Yes!' said Demelza. 'Very special! It— Ow!' she yelled as the pickled knight head-butted her shin.

'– was my father's!' he finished for her. 'It was all I had to remember him by. I'll forgive you for stealing it – and everything else - if you just tell us where that cup is.'

The ghost twirled his ragged beard as he strolled back to them. He didn't look as though he believed the story, but he suddenly seemed a lot more interested in talking to them.

'I don't need your forgiveness for nothin',' said the ghost. 'But I'll tell you what happened to the cup.' He leant forwards, eyes wide as he whispered. 'SHE took it. I was trying to sell it in the market square and this swan swoops down out of the air and snatches it. I know it was one of HERS.'

'Who's SHE?' asked Nessa.

The pickled knight sighed. 'SHE is the Lady of the Lake.'

Chapter Eight
TRESPASSING

'The Lady of the Lake?' Demelza scratched her chin. 'Like in the story? The one where the king bloke has his sword chucked in the water and a hand pops up an' grabs it?'

'I don't know about that,' said the ghost. 'We calls her that cos she lives on one of them little islands in the middle of the lake. Never leaves neither, but the island is always green, even in winter.'

'She's still here?' said the pickled knight. 'After all these years? Then she DOES have my cup!'

'And if it's kept someone alive for hundreds of years, then it really can help Honkers!'

Demelza grabbed Nessa's hands and did a little happy dance. 'What are we waiting for? Let's go!'

'Halt your prancing!' scowled the pickled knight. 'This will be more dangerous than I expected. The Lady and the Penfurzy knights were not on the best of terms.'

'Why's that?' asked Nessa.

The pickled knight gave a very good shrug for someone without shoulders. 'Well, she had a problem with us for some reason or other.'

'Was it to do with you charging off to other countries, bossing their people about and stealing all their treasures?'

The pickled knight shrugged again. 'Who knows. Women can be so— umph!' His sentence ended with Nessa's boot in his mouth.

'Just going to stop you there, Pickles,' said Nessa. 'I reckon me and the Lady will get on just fine.'

The pickled knight spat out a lump of swamp mud as Nessa removed her foot. Demelza picked him up by the ears and popped him into her own basket before he said anything else to annoy Nessa.

'Not far to go now,' she said as they continued their journey over the viaduct, glad that their chance meeting with Margh had at least saved time searching for him. 'The lake is a few miles thataway. We can get there by midnight if we're quick.'

A green glow followed them as they cleared the viaduct. Demelza looked over her shoulder. The straggly ghost was floating after them.

'Can we help you?' asked Nessa.

'Thought I'd join you,' smirked the ghost. 'If my cup is as special as you say it is, maybe it can make me solid again.'

'MY cup!' shouted the pickled knight. 'It's not yours. You stole it from *me!*'

'And you stole it from a dead dude,' said Nessa, 'which is the whole point of us trying to return it.'

'*After* we save Honkers,' said Demelza. 'And, um, I'm sorry, Mr Ghostie, but I reckon the water from the cup has to touch you for it to work, and you don't have all the bits you need for drinking.'

'Of course I can drink—' the ghost started to argue.

Nessa took a bottle of water out of her bag and threw it to him. 'Think fast!' The bottle went straight through the ghost and landed on the tracks. 'Sorry, dude,' she said as Margh's hand passed through the bottle every time he tried to pick it up. 'D's right. It won't work for you.'

The ghost stroked his beard. 'Ah well,' he said at last, 'who wants to be solid anyway? You can't do *this*!' And Demelza felt a tickly chill in her stomach as the ghost ran through them all whooping gleefully. 'Say hello to the Lady for me. I'm off to see who else has popped into town this evening. I met a lovely Victorian gal at the bandstand a few years back. I wonder if she's in town tonight?' He tossed his beard over his shoulder and skipped off down the track. 'Catch you all later, dead or alive.'

'Dead or alive? What did he mean by that?' said Demelza as they began to roll downhill.

'Oh, nothing,' the pickled knight called back, his hair streaming back in the wind as they hurtled down the sloping trail. 'I'm sure she has mellowed by now.'

Demelza took a big glug of cherryade, then wiped her stained red lips with the back of her hand. 'Not far,' she burped. 'The lake is just over this ridge.'

'And how do you propose to get out to the island?' asked the pickled knight, wriggling out of the basket and rolling over to them. 'I don't suppose you have a boat in those sacks?'

Demelza smacked herself on the forehead. She hadn't thought of that. She even had a rubber dingy under the caravan, but there was no time to cycle back for it, not if they wanted to get home in time to save Honkers. But how could they get the cup without a boat? The lake was far too deep and cold to swim across. She felt as though her head was going to explode.

'It's a lake,' said Nessa. 'Isn't there somewhere that hires out boats?'

'Yes. They have rowing boats, kayaks and pedalos. But it's nearly midnight, so no one's going to be there now. As it's an emergency, maybe it would be OK if we borrowed one and put it back, but they'll be locked up and we can't break in.'

'Then it's a good job you're with the world's greatest lock picker,' said Nessa. 'Nothing needs to get broken and no one will even know we were there. Did I tell you about the time I escaped from a prison island in the middle of the Arctic Ocean?'

'Only twice,' said Demelza, getting up and brushing crumbs from her anorak. 'OK, as long as we come back and pay to rent a boat during the day.'

'Very noble,' grumbled the pickled knight, 'but can we please get moving?'

'Come on then,' said Demelza firmly, 'To the boathouse!'

The lake was silent and still as they cycled down to the shore and followed it towards the boathouse. The moon glinted off the ink-black water, picking out the dark islands in the centre. Demelza had been out rowing with her dad, but no one ever landed on the islands as they were home to a bevy of angry swans. Was there really a woman, hundreds of years old, living on one of them?

The boathouse stood on a platform at the edge of the lake, jetties stretching out over the water at either side. It was shut up when they reached it. The windows were protected with metal mesh and there was a thick chain with a padlock holding the doors closed.

'Right then,' Nessa flexed her fingers and stepped onto the ramp that sloped down from the doors to the lake. 'Let's get trespassing!' She unfastened two of the many safety pins decorating her denim jacket, pulled them straight and slid one into the bottom of the lock.

'What is she doing?' asked the pickled knight, standing still to keep his head torch focused on her as she worked on the padlock. Demelza held her breath. Every year she tried picking the lock on the trunk where her dad stored her Christmas presents but had never managed it. Would Nessa really be able to pick the lock? There were lots of little metallic clicks, and frustrated grunts from Nessa, but finally she let out a whoop as the open padlock dropped with a thunk. She unwrapped the heavy chain from around the door handles and let it jangle to the floor.

'You did it!' said Demelza, jumping up and down as she gave her a hug. 'You're the best!'

'Well done, Trespasser!' said the pickled knight, bouncing into the boathouse as the girls pulled open the doors. His head torch sent creepy shadows dancing around the walls.

Nessa rubbed her hands together as she looked around. The boathouse was filled with boats of all shapes and sizes. Kayaks on racks on the walls, rowing boats overturned in neat rows around the sides of the room, and in the middle . . .

'The pedalos!' breathed Demelza, patting the beak of one of the huge, swan-shaped pedal boats.

'Which one shall we take?' asked Demelza.

'That one,' said Nessa.

Demelza gasped as Nessa heaved aside the white pedalos to reveal a green one painted with scales and red, clawed wings.

'A dragon,' breathed Demelza, stroking its long neck. The gold specks in its yellow eyes glinted in the light of her torch. 'Perfect!'

PEDALO
enjoy!
FUN

Chapter Nine

THE LADY OF THE LAKE

‘What manner of craft is this?’ asked the pickled knight as Demelza placed him on the little ledge between the two plastic seats then helped Nessa shove the dragon pedalo down the ramp and into the lake with a SPLOOSH!

‘The best kind,’ said Demelza as she hopped into one of the seats and put her feet on the pedals. ‘A boat you ride like a bike!’

‘What else would the Penfurzy Rebel Bicycle Club sail in?’ said Nessa as she jumped in the other side and bumped fists with Demelza.

‘And the members of this club are . . . ?’ asked the pickled knight.

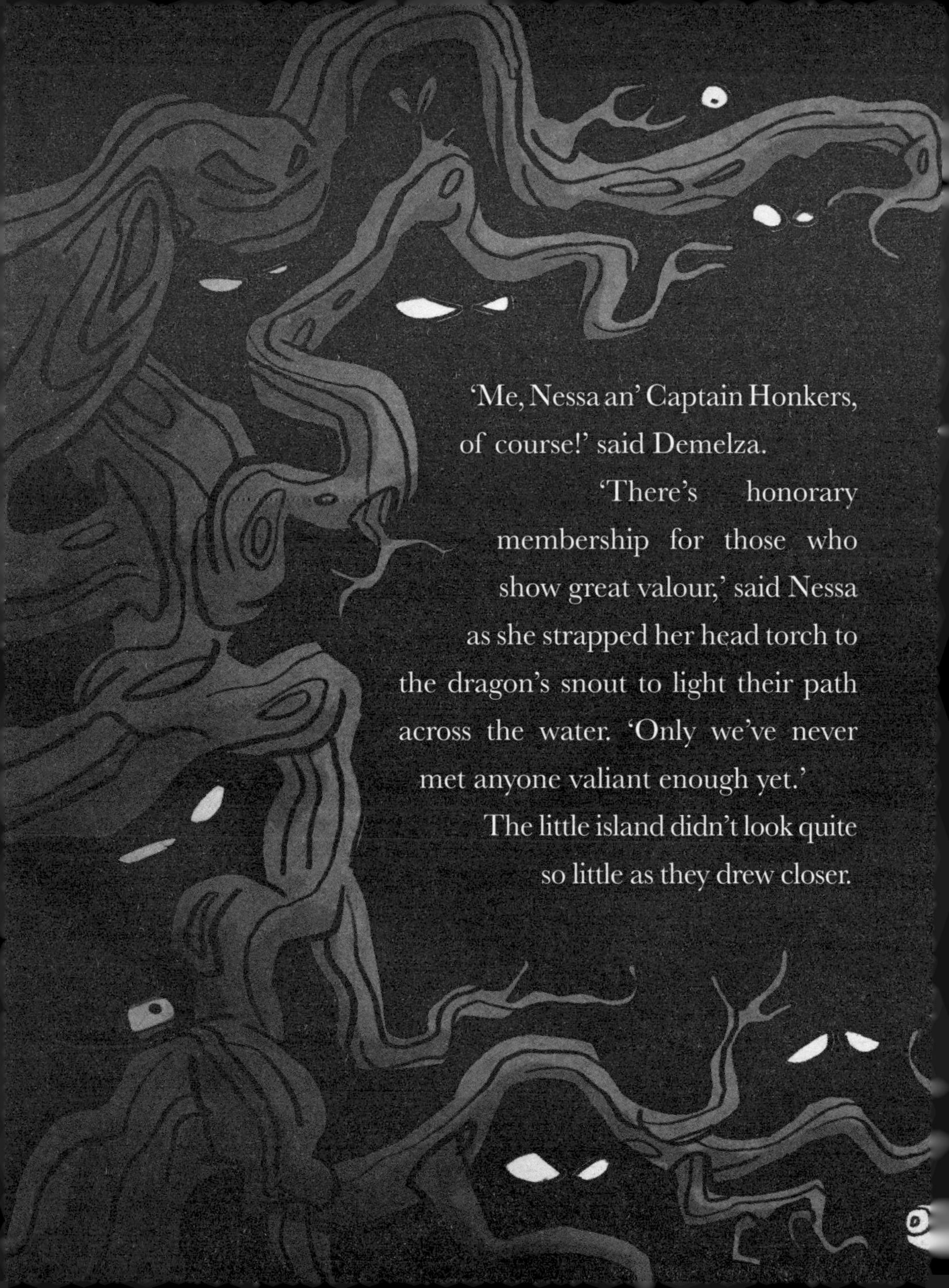

'Me, Nessa an' Captain Honkers, of course!' said Demelza.

'There's honorary membership for those who show great valour,' said Nessa as she strapped her head torch to the dragon's snout to light their path across the water. 'Only we've never met anyone valiant enough yet.'

The little island didn't look quite so little as they drew closer.

Tree roots slithered into the water like sea serpents - or giant squid tentacles reaching out for them. Hundreds of beady bird eyes glinted in the torchlight, watching from their nests among the roots as the girls sailed their dragon up to the island.

'Land ho!' said Nessa, jumping onto the shore and looping the rope that hung from the dragon's neck around a tree trunk. The pickled knight hopped down onto the island and Demelza followed him, trying not to look at all the eyes following them – and especially not at the swans who looked like little ghosts drifting silently over the black water, feathers glowing in the moonlight.

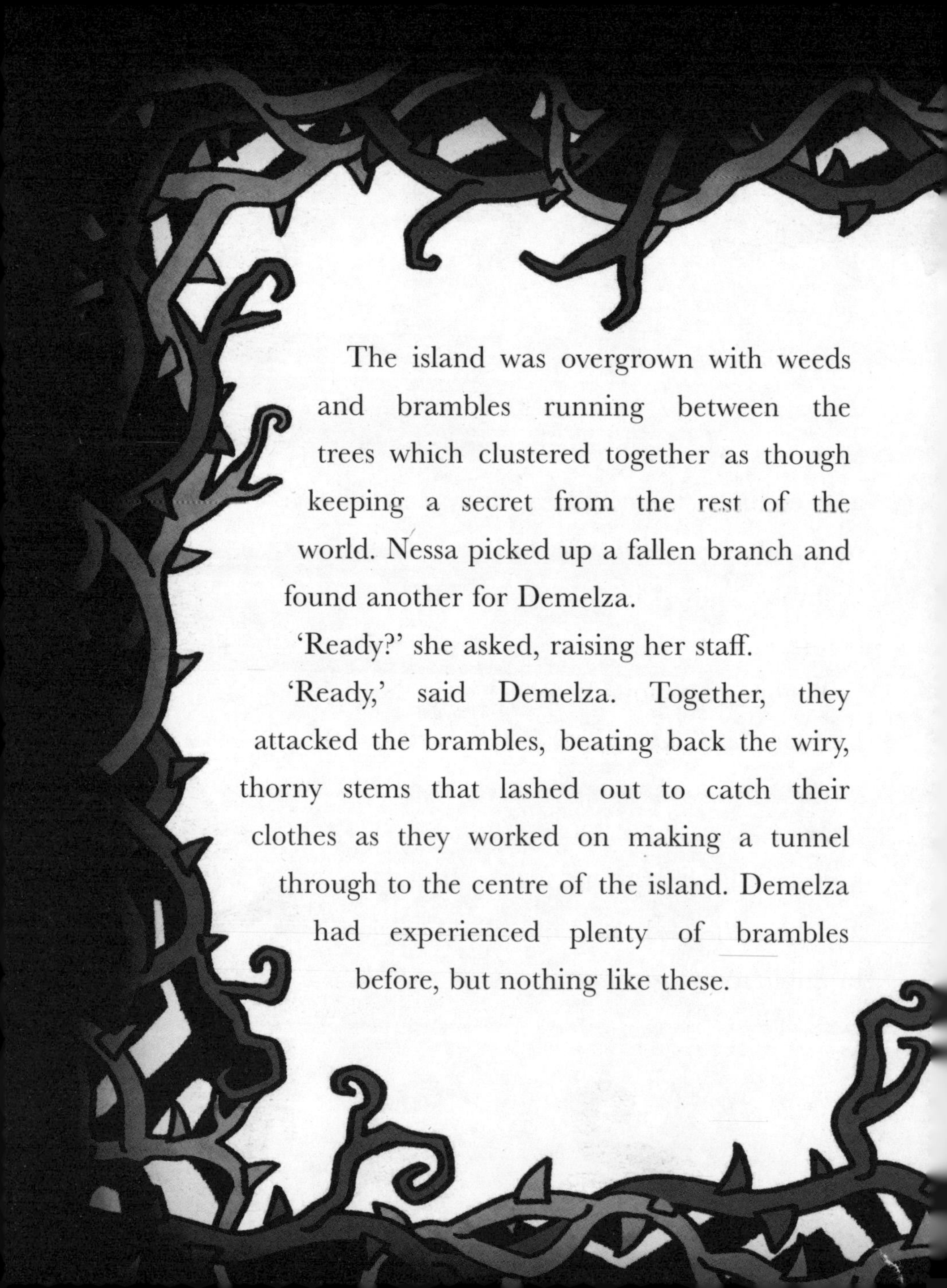

The island was overgrown with weeds and brambles running between the trees which clustered together as though keeping a secret from the rest of the world. Nessa picked up a fallen branch and found another for Demelza.

'Ready?' she asked, raising her staff.

'Ready,' said Demelza. Together, they attacked the brambles, beating back the wiry, thorny stems that lashed out to catch their clothes as they worked on making a tunnel through to the centre of the island. Demelza had experienced plenty of brambles before, but nothing like these.

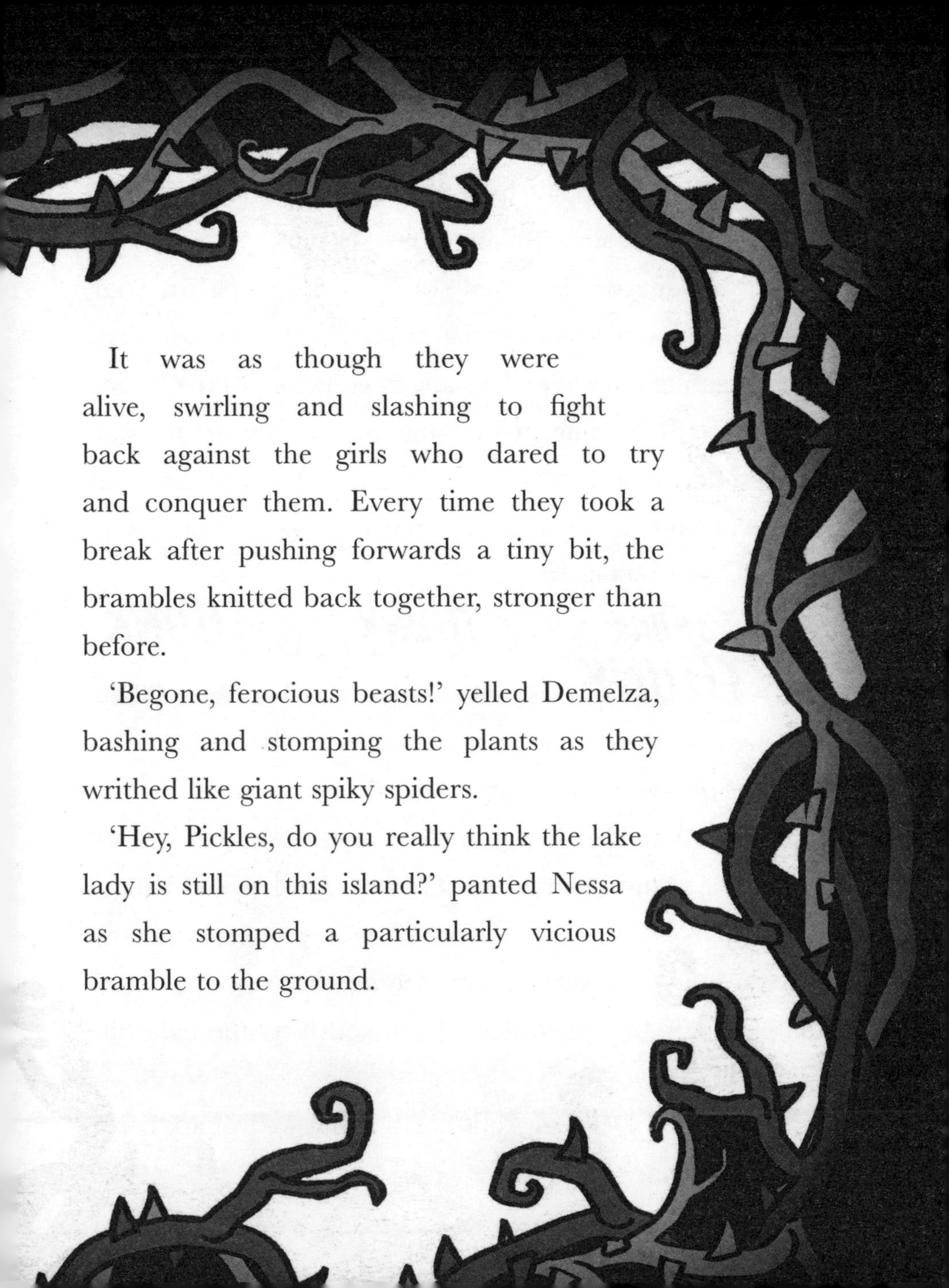

It was as though they were alive, swirling and slashing to fight back against the girls who dared to try and conquer them. Every time they took a break after pushing forwards a tiny bit, the brambles knitted back together, stronger than before.

'Begone, ferocious beasts!' yelled Demelza, bashing and stomping the plants as they writhed like giant spiky spiders.

'Hey, Pickles, do you really think the lake lady is still on this island?' panted Nessa as she stomped a particularly vicious bramble to the ground.

'I'm sure of it,' said the pickled knight, bouncing from side to side to avoid the whipping brambles and the girls' flailing staffs. 'Look at how hard she's working to keep us out.'

After working on the brambles for at least half an hour, Demelza threw her staff to the ground with a growl. They weren't getting anywhere. Nessa kept going for a little longer, grunting and shouting at the stubborn bushes as her staff thunked down on them again and again. Her spiky hair was stuck to her forehead with sweat and her cheeks and hands were covered in tiny scratches.

'Why' - ***THUNK*** - 'won't' - ***THUNK*** - 'you'- ***THUNK*** - 'die?' - ***THUNK*** - she yelled, before dropping the staff and flopping onto the ground next to Demelza. 'We need another plan,' she sighed.

Demelza licked her hanky and wiped her face, then offered it to Nessa, then picked at a scab on her knee as she thought hard.

'Keep trying!' shouted the pickled knight from atop a tree stump. 'Come back with axes. Burn your way through! She *will* yield!'

'Maybe,' said Demelza, 'but how's about we just ask her if we can come in?'

'Ask?' said the pickled knight. 'ASK?! Nobody just *asks* the Lady of the Lake for an audience. Men have been gravely injured in their attempts to get an audience with her.'

'Did any of those men try asking nicely?' said Nessa, picking thorns out of her jeans.

The pickled knight's eyebrows shot up so quickly his eyeballs nearly popped out again. 'Of course not!' he snorted.

'Betcha that's where they went wrong,' said Nessa. 'Want to give it a go, D?'

Demelza stood up and cupped her hands around her mouth. 'Hellooooo!' she called, then paused to listen for a reply.

The island was quiet other than the chittering of bats and sleepy quacking of ducks, but Demelza could feel it was listening. She shivered as she noticed the swans had drifted over to line the shore behind them, as though to stop them leaving.

'We seek an audience with the Lady of the Lake,' called Nessa.

Silence.

'Enough talk!' The pickled knight bounced on his tree stump. 'Force beats fancy talk. Take up your weapons! Fight your way through!'

The trees swayed as though the island had breathed out. Tiny bats swooped from the branches and away over the lake as dry leaves rustled against each other and showered down onto the girls.

'Who dares trespass here?' whispered a voice that sounded as old and dry as the dead leaves.

'Nessa, Demelza and, er, guest,' said Demelza. 'We'd like to speak to you, your Lady of the Lakeship, if you don't mind. Thank you very much. Please.'

'I do not know you,' said the voice, 'and I speak to no one.' Demelza decided not to point out she was speaking to them right now.

'Surely even you have heard tales of the Imp and the Trespasser? Castle-crashers, curse-breakers, riders of iron steeds?'

'Aluminium,' whispered Nessa. 'An iron bike would go rusty.'

'An' it would be dead heavy!' added Demelza.

'Sir Calenick?' said the voice. 'You roam Penfurzy still? I felt the breaking of the curse you and your brother knights had brought upon our land. Why didn't you leave with them?'

'We-lllll, that's what we've come to see you about,' said the pickled knight. 'It's about the cup. The one you took from Mad Margh.'

The voice was silent for a few moments, then the trees and brambles in front of them shook and shuddered.

'Whoa!' said Nessa as Demelza watched the brambles untangle and weave themselves into an arched tunnel, a tunnel leading straight to the heart of the island.

'Enter, Imp, Trespasser and disembodied knight,' said the voice.

Demelza took Nessa's hand and they entered the tunnel, keeping an eye out for stray brambles that might try to take a swipe at them, but they were all very well behaved now. The pickled knight hopped slowly after them, as though nervous to meet the owner of the voice.

Nessa let out a whistle as they stepped into a clearing where brambles and vines had wrapped themselves around the trees, forming arches and ornate patterns.

'It's like a cathedral!' said Demelza, looking up at the dome of branches. There was a perfectly round hole in the centre through which the full moon shone down into a stone basin of water next to a big mossy rock. No, not a rock. Demelza looked again. Rocks didn't move.

A white arm splotched with dark age spots reached out from under the brown moss-covered cloak which Demelza had mistaken for a rock. It was holding a wooden cup shaped like a large wine glass. Was this the cup they were looking for? The one that could save Captain Honkers? The hand dipped the cup into the basin to fill it, then withdrew into the cloak. Demelza looked up at Nessa. Slurping sounds were coming from under the cloak.

'Must be thirsty work, controlling a living island,' shrugged Nessa.

The slurping finally stopped. A soft glow began seeping out from under the cloak. Demelza gasped and grasped Nessa's arm as the rock stood up. The mossy cloak slid to the ground and the glow filled the whole clearing. Demelza and Nessa covered their eyes and blinked as the sudden light after hours of darkness blinded them for a moment.

The light faded and they removed their hands to see a woman standing in front of them. She wore a dress woven from moss and long grass, which Demelza thought surprisingly beautiful. Her long silver-streaked black hair flowed down to the ground. The age spots on her pale arms had gone and she was looking at them with silver eyes that Demelza was sure were looking right into her mind and seeing every naughty thing she had ever done then tried to blame on Captain Honkers.

'The Lady of the Lake,' sighed Nessa, dropping to one knee in front of her. Demelza copied her and saw a little smile appear at the corner of the woman's dark lips.

'Well, Imp, Trespasser. You have come for the cup,' said the Lady. 'The cup which has sustained me for hundreds of years. Tell me why I shouldn't cast your bodies into the cold, dark depths of the lake to rest with all the other souls who have come seeking it.'

Chapter Ten
THE PENDRAGON CUP

Demelza stared at the Lady and scratched her chin. She really didn't want to be cast into the cold, dark depths of the lake. Especially if there were a load of mouldy old skeletons already down there.

'We need it to heal Captain Honkers,' she said at last. 'He's my friend. The bravest, most loyal, kindest friend in the whole wide world. Besides Nessa,' she added quickly.

'You wish to heal your friend and then return the cup to me?' said the Lady.

'Not exactly . . .' said Nessa. 'You see, it's not your cup. Pickles . . . I mean Sir Calenick, pinched it from the tomb of an ancient king. We need to return it so that he can go . . . well, wherever it is people go when they're done living.'

'And are you?'

the Lady asked the pickled knight who was skulking behind Nessa and Demelza's legs.

He finally shuffled himself forwards and met her piercing eyes. 'Am I what?'

'Done living,' she replied.

He tilted his head to one side and paused for a moment. 'I suppose I am,' he said at last. 'I spent centuries with nobody to talk to. The world is a strange place now.'

Demelza gulped down a laugh at the 'no body' comment and tried not to look at Nessa whose shoulders were shaking a little.

'Strange indeed,' said the Lady with a sigh. She sat down and beckoned them over. 'Come, sit.' Demelza and Nessa sat down cross-legged opposite her as the pickled knight nestled into a comfy bed of moss. The Lady clapped her hands. Weasels and squirrels ran out of the trees and bushes and laid a little picnic of nuts and berries on the ground between them. Demelza opened her lunch box and added some cheese, crackers, chocolate, tomato sauce sandwiches and pickled onion crisps to the feast.

'Thank you,' said Nessa, trying to take a hazelnut that a squirrel was offering but didn't seem to want to let go of.

'Few people believe in me these days,' said the Lady as the girls tucked into the feast. 'If I give you the cup, I must return to the lake and leave this world. If I am to do that, I must be sure that you are worthy to take it, and that you will keep your word to return the cup to its owner.'

'We promise. Cross our hearts and hope to die,' said Demelza, wiping berry juice from her mouth with the back of her hand.

'Stick hot needles in our eyes,' added Nessa.

'There is no need for hot needles,' said the Lady. 'But I do need a stronger promise. If I am to give you the cup, I must take one of you with me as payment when I slip below the waters.'

Demelza gulped. 'You know we can't breathe underwater, right?' The Lady's expression didn't change. 'Oh, she already knows that,' she whispered to Nessa.

Nessa stepped forwards. 'I'll go with you. If you give Demelza the cup to save Captain Honkers, then I'll go with you.'

'Even if that means you will never see her again?' said the Lady.

'Yes,' said Nessa, raising her chin. 'Even if that's what it means.'

Demelza felt hot and cold and tearful and shivery all at the same time. 'No!' she burst out. 'You can't take Nessa away for ever. I'll go with you. Nessa, you take the cup back. Use it to save Captain Honkers and then look after him and Dad.'

'No way,' said Nessa. 'I'm staying here. You should be the first thing Honkers sees when he wakes up. He needs you. And so does your dad.'

'But what about your parents?' said Demelza. 'What would I tell them? No! I'm staying, you take the cup. I—'

'Neither of you will stay,' boomed a voice from knee height. The pickled knight jumped forwards and stared up at the Lady. 'I will go with you, and these two brave knights will save their goose and return the cup to its rightful place.'

The Lady raised her hands. The clearing was silent for a moment.

'Your captain is . . . a goose? Each one of you would sacrifice themselves for the others?' she asked. 'All for the life of a goose?'

Demelza, Nessa and the pickled knight nodded together.

'Captain Honkers is the bravest goose in the world,' said Nessa. 'His life is no less important than any of ours.'

The Lady nodded. 'Then I shall make the choice for you. She tapped her finger on her lips as she stared at them for what seemed like for ever. 'And I choose . . .'

Demelza held her breath. She really didn't want to live below the cold dark boating lake for ever, but if that was what it took to save Captain Honkers . . .

'None of you,' said the Lady. 'You have all shown bravery and loyalty to your fellow knights. Such true souls should be rewarded.' She reached into the folds of her dress, drew out the cup and offered it to Demelza, who decided it was a good time to start breathing again. She took hold of the cup but the Lady didn't let go. She looked Demelza in the eyes.

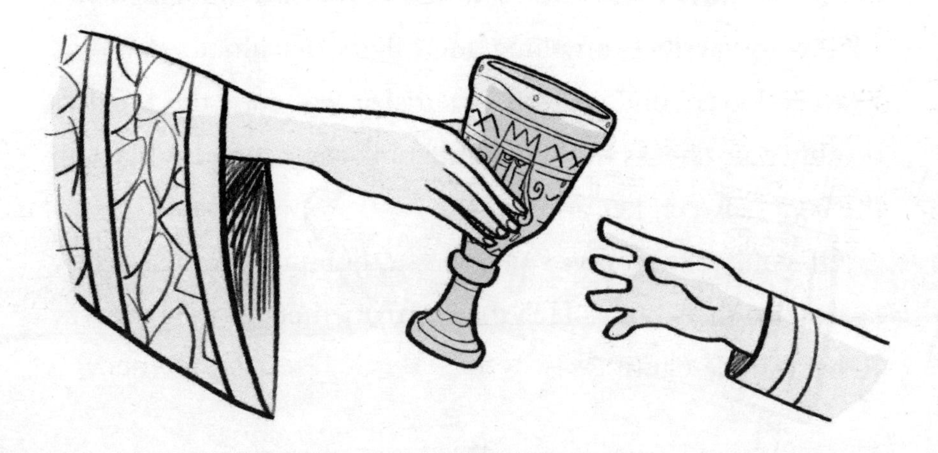

'Use it wisely. Its power is addictive. I have used it for too long. When you have saved your friend, be sure to return it to King Pendragon's tomb as you have promised.' She let go of the cup at last.

'Thank you,' said Demelza. She tucked the cup into her backpack as she tried to remember where she had heard the name Pendragon before.

'Without the cup, you won't be able to stay here?' asked Nessa.

The Lady shrugged. 'I've already stayed in this realm too long. Time to move on.' She followed them through the green tunnel that led back to their dragon boat, the pickled knight bouncing along behind her. 'You have grown, Sir Calenick,' she said as Nessa helped him into the boat. 'Not in stature, but in the ways that count. I would never have imagined you willing to sacrifice anything for others, let alone your life. Bravery looks good on you.' Demelza was sure the knight's deathly pale cheeks flushed a little pink as he took his place in the boat between her and Nessa.

'Of course he's brave,' said Nessa, bumping her fist gently against his cheekbone. 'He's the fourth member of the Penfurzy Rebel Bicycle Club!'

Demelza was sure the tiniest of smiles tickled at the corner of the pickled knight's mouth as they began to pedal away from the island. The Lady walked out into the lake alongside their dragon craft, her long hair and dress swirling in the water.

'What are you doing?' asked Nessa. 'You'll drown, get in here.' She reached out her arm to help her climb aboard, but the Lady gently pushed it away.

'It's OK,' she said, smiling at them as she stopped with the water at her chest. 'I'm going home. Safe travels, brave friends.' She glanced over her shoulder. 'I have an honour guard . . .' she added softly, and Nessa gasped as she could see swan after swan after swan gliding in a V-formation towards where the Lady waited.

'Thank you!' Demelza waved to her as they pedalled their dragon away from the island and towards the shore.

'And thank you for the cup!' called Nessa.

'And for not drowning us!' added Demelza.

The Lady waved back, then slowly slid beneath the dark water until all that could be seen was her raised arm, skin shining silver in the moonlight, until that too slid down into the silent black lake and the swans bowed their heads mournfully and sailed away into the night.

Chapter Eleven
SAVING CAPTAIN HONKERS

Nessa chained up the doors of the boathouse again after they returned the dragon pedalo, then pressed the little light button on the side of her calculator watch.

'It's nearly three now, so if we get pedalling we'll be back before dawn.'

'Hold on, Honkers,' said Demelza as they jumped on their bikes. 'We're coming!'

The cycle home took forever. Demelza and Nessa rode most of the way in silence, checking the time every ten minutes.

The pickled knight shouted encouragement from Nessa's basket as they rode, delighted by his admittance into the Penfurzy Rebel Bicycle Club, but even he grew tired and fell silent as the night wore on and the world whizzed by. Around the lake, up the hill, over the viaduct, along the rail tracks, through the woods, skirting the marsh, across the fields and along the cliff tops. Demelza had been thinking hard all the way.

'Nessa . . .'

'Yeah?'

'What do you think comes next? You know, when we die?'

'That's a big question, D.' Nessa was quiet for a while. 'Are you thinking about Captain Honkers?'

Demelza swallowed down a lump that came up into her throat. 'A bit. And . . . Mum. I wonder if she's wherever the Lady went?'

'Maybe it's different for everyone, depending what you believe,' said Nessa. 'What do you think happens?'

Demelza shrugged. 'Dunno. But . . . I'd like it if she could see me from wherever she is.'

'I'm sure she can,' said Nessa, 'and I bet she's happy you're having your own adventures.'

Demelza smiled and rubbed her nose. 'I think so too.'

All the lights were on in the house when they finally reached the golf course and caravan park.

'That's the vet's car!' Demelza yelped. They dropped their bikes, scooped the pickled knight up into Nessa's backpack and ran for the house.

'We're too late!' wailed Demelza as they ran into the kitchen. The vet and Demelza's dad were leaning over Captain Honkers who was lying on a big cushion on the kitchen table. The vet's face was serious.

'Demelza!' said her dad as she rushed to the goose's side. Honkers looked up at her, too weak to raise his head and honk. 'I didn't want to wake you. I'm sorry. It doesn't look good.' He put his arm around her.

Demelza shook it off as she cradled Captain Honkers' head. 'How could you not wake me?' she demanded, ignoring the fact that she hadn't even been in the caravan to be woken up. Tears burned her eyes and fell onto the goose's broken feathers.

'I'm sorry, Demelza,' said her dad, stroking her shoulder then looking puzzled at the amount of mud flaking off her clothes and onto the floor. 'You're here now. We can say goodbye together.'

'No one is saying goodbye,' said Demelza, 'cos no one is dying. Not today.' She pulled the cup from her backpack and threw it to Nessa who filled it under the kitchen tap.

'Demelza . . .' said her dad.

'Don't Demelza me,' she said, pulling away from him as she took the cup from Nessa. She held it to Captain Honkers' beak. 'Come on, Honkers, just a little sip,' she whispered, raising his head with the other hand. The goose didn't even try. Demelza's whole body shook with a giant sob. 'He can't drink!' she said, burying her head in Nessa's jacket. 'How can we save him if he can't drink?'

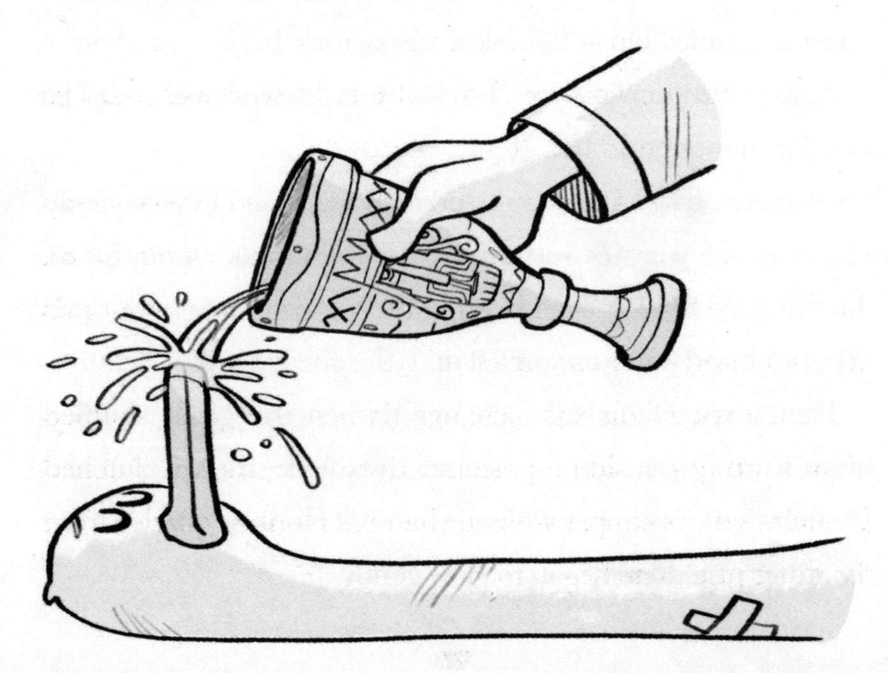

'I'm sorry,' said the vet, 'but he needs more than water to save him. It would take a miracle, and there aren't many of those around.'

'We've got a miracle!' sobbed Demelza. 'It's just not working.' Nessa gently moved Demelza into her dad's arms and rummaged through her backpack, being very careful not to put her fingers up the pickled knight's nose as she searched.

'Got it!' She pulled a blue plastic gun out of her bag, grabbed the cup and poured the water into a little hole at the top of the toy.

'A water pistol?' Demelza rubbed her eyes and nose on her dad's sleeve. 'What are you going to— Ohhhhhh! Nessa, you're a genius! Do you think it will work?'

'The water touched the cup, so I reckon whatever happens to it has happened,' said Nessa. 'Ready?'

Demelza lifted Captain Honkers' head and Nessa gently squeezed the trigger to begin squirting water down his throat. The vet and Demelza's dad watched with sad faces as the girls kept dribbling water into his beak.

Their expressions soon changed when the goose shuffled himself up into a sitting position. Eyes wide, the vet clutched Demelza's dad's jumper with one hand as Honkers guzzled from the water pistol and began to glow gently.

'It's working!' shouted Demelza.

'Quick, more water!' said Nessa as the last few drops ran down Captain Honkers' throat. He began bobbing his head for more.

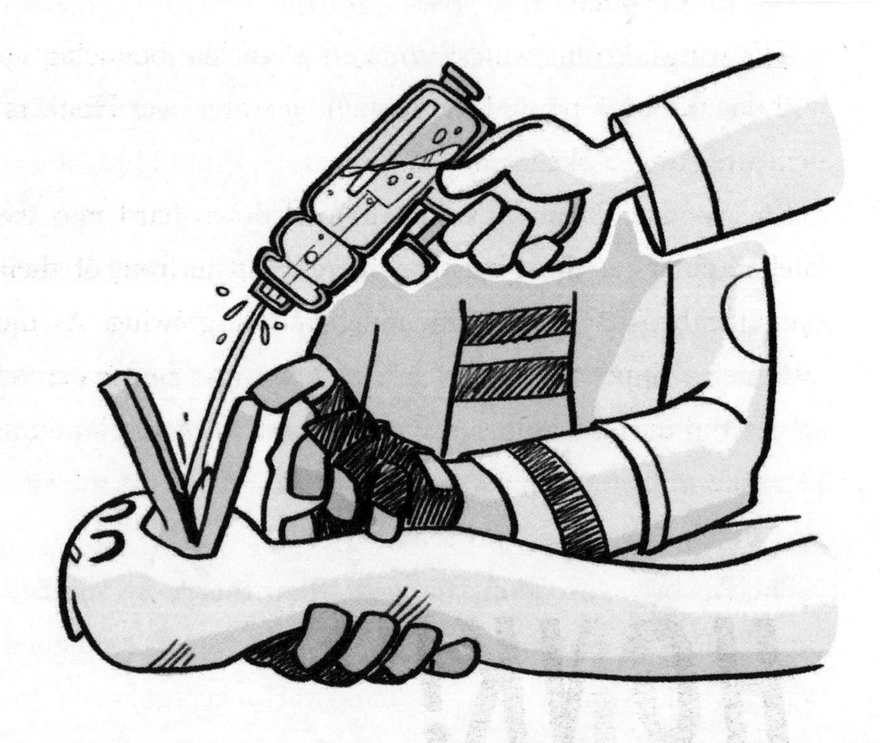

‘I’m coming, Honkers!’ said Demelza, running to the sink to refill the wooden cup. ‘Drink it all up!’ The goose plunged his beak into the cup, bobbing his head up and down as he swallowed gulp after gulp. When he finally finished, Nessa took the cup and poured the rest of the water over his wounds - first over the red puncture marks in his neck from General Barkley’s teeth, which bubbled and fizzed white then disappeared completely.

‘His wings, do his wings!’ shouted Demelza, bouncing up and down. Nessa poured the remaining water over Honkers’ bent wing and broken feathers.

The vet and Demelza’s dad flopped down hard into the kitchen chairs as the wing straightened out in front of their eyes, the broken feathers mending and re-growing. As the last drop dripped onto his feathers, Captain Honkers stood tall, raised his perfect wings, flapped them hard and let out a gigantic:

HONK!

HONK!

Demelza threw her arms around Nessa and they bounced excitedly around the kitchen before performing the Penfurzy Rebel Bicycle Club handshake whilst whooping with joy. Captain Honkers flew over to join in the celebration, running around the kitchen, great wings raised as he honked louder than ever before:

Honk, HONK, HOOOOOOOONK!

'I don't believe it,' said the vet when it was finally quiet enough for her make herself heard over the celebrations. 'I've never seen a recovery like it. Never! What did you give him?'

'Water,' laughed Demelza as she touched her fingers to Captain Honkers' wing tips and danced with him. 'Just ordinary water from the kitchen tap.'

The vet took the cup, turned it over in her hand and then put it back on the table. 'Well, it seems I'm not needed here,' she said, watching Captain Honkers race around after the girls as if he were a gosling again. 'I've never seen such a healthy goose in my life.' She shook hands with Demelza's dad, then put her coat on inside out. 'Just one thing before I leave, Gryff . . .' She picked up the cup. 'I wouldn't mind a drink of water.'

They all flopped onto the sofa as the vet's headlights flashed through the windows as she swung her car around and headed off back to town.

'Well, that was strange,' said Demelza's dad as Captain Honkers bounced from knee to knee. 'I know our kitchen water doesn't do anything special, otherwise I wouldn't still have such a bad back from my roadie days. What else did you put in that cup?'

'Nothing,' said Demelza. 'It really was just water. It's a magic cup!' She filled it again and held it out to her dad. 'Try it.'

He took the cup, sniffed the contents, then took a sip. Demelza grinned as he straightened up, eyes wide as he rolled his shoulders and twisted from side to side.

'Where would you find a magic cup?' he gasped, turning it over in his hands and examining it closely. 'It doesn't look anything special, but you two – you look like a couple of mud monsters. Which is very strange, considering you've been tucked up in the caravan all night.'

'Ummmmmmmmm,' said Demelza, looking at Nessa as her mind whirred searching for an explanation. 'We, ummmmmmmmmm . . .'

'A friend said we could borrow it to help Captain Honkers, Mr Penrose,' said Nessa quickly. 'Then we're taking it back to where it belongs. It's called the Pendragon Cup.'

The cup flew out of his hands as if it was coated in butter. Demelza leapt to grab it.

'The Pendragon Cup? THE Pendragon Cup?' He took the cup back gently and gazed at it as if it was a precious jewel. 'It can't be. Demelza, your mother's notebooks, go get them from your room.'

Demelza sprinted upstairs, pulled a cardboard box from under her bed and hurried back down with it. Her dad had given her the notebooks after she found the treasure of the Penfurzy knights with Nessa, but she hadn't had time to look through them properly yet. She dropped the box on the living-room rug.

'Find the Pendragon one.'

Nessa flumped onto the floor next to Demelza and they began pulling out the notebooks. Each featured an exciting title in Demelza's mum's beautiful handwriting:

And many more.

'Ooh! Here's it is,' said Nessa, shoving a notebook into Demelza's hands. 'The Pendragon Puzzle.'

Demelza ran her finger over her mum's looping letters and opened the cover. On the very first page was a drawing of the very cup they had brought back from the Lady of the Lake.

Underneath were the words:

The magical cup of Penfurzy's greatest king, rumoured to lie with his body within the Great Barrow on Penfurzy island where, legend says, he is sleeping a magical sleep until the land's need is so great that he will rise again to defend it.

Nessa rested her chin on Demelza's shoulder. 'Does she say anything about where the Great Barrow is?' she asked.

Demelza flipped through pages of beautifully drawn maps and notes on all of the clues Demelza's mum had explored. 'Here!' she said at last, stabbing her finger onto the final page. '"The Great Barrow lies just outside town in the middle of Penfurzy island." She says something was built on top of it in 1967.'

‘What?’ asked Nessa. ‘Houses? A school? The pasty factory?’

Demelza shook her head. She pulled a leaflet out of the back of the notebook and unfolded it to reveal a brightly coloured map of a strange and wonderful land.

‘Piskie Parc!’ whispered Demelza. ‘The bestest, funnest funfair in all of the world!’

TALKING
HEADS

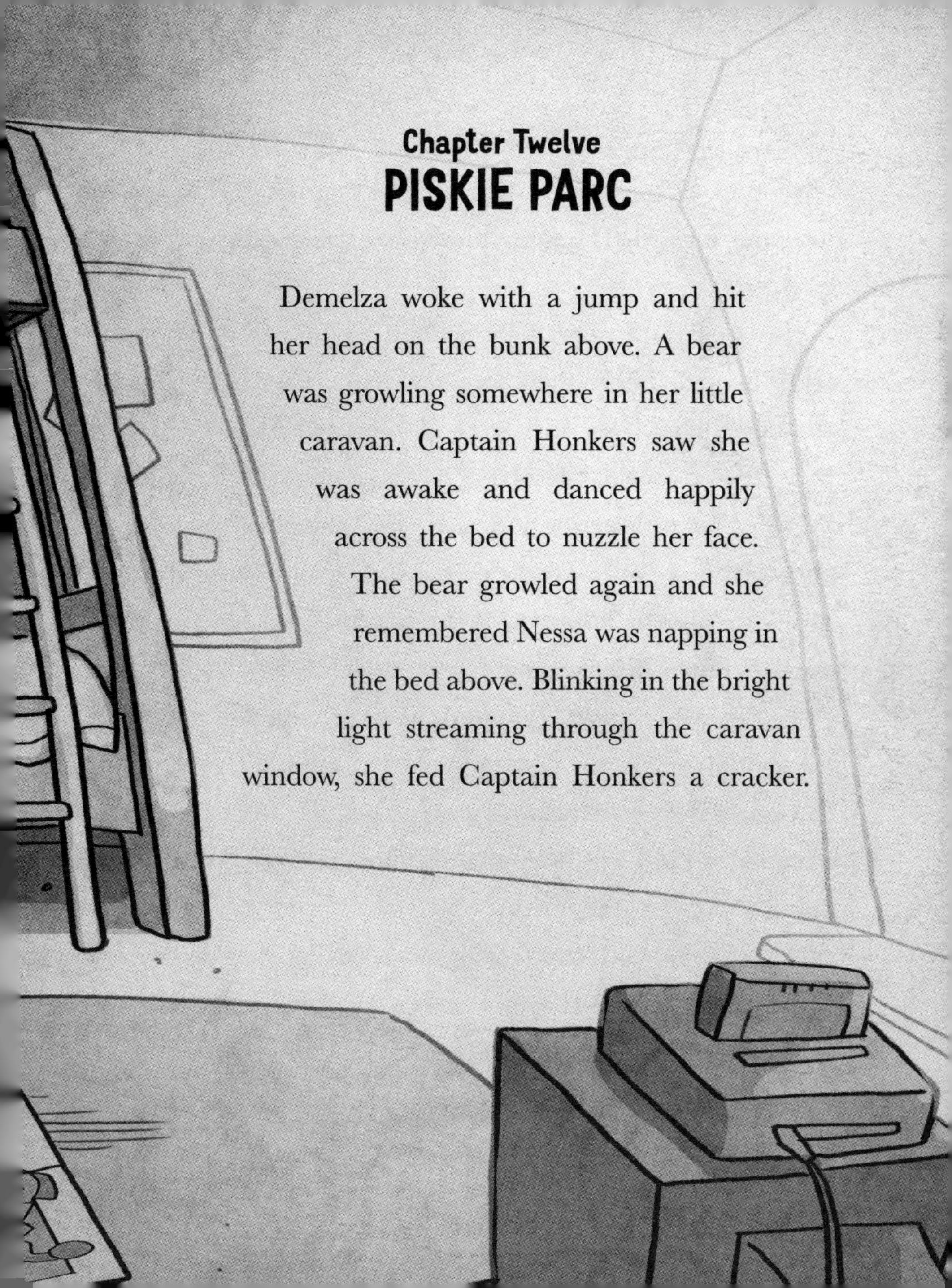

Chapter Twelve
PISKIE PARC

Demelza woke with a jump and hit her head on the bunk above. A bear was growling somewhere in her little caravan. Captain Honkers saw she was awake and danced happily across the bed to nuzzle her face. The bear growled again and she remembered Nessa was napping in the bed above. Blinking in the bright light streaming through the caravan window, she fed Captain Honkers a cracker.

They had slept the whole morning away after their night-time adventure. Demelza was very grateful that her dad had been too amazed with Honkers' incredible recovery to ask many questions.

She opened the map of Piskie Parc and spread it out on the bed. She hadn't been there for a few years. The park was quite run-down now. The rides were all a bit rickety and Connan had told everyone at school that he had got the plague from the Whizzy Watersplash ride and had to take a week off school. The park was also closed for the winter, so if they were going to return the cup to the Great Barrow, they'd have to sneak in. Somehow, she didn't think Nessa would have a problem with that.

'You're awake at last!' shouted the pickled knight, rolling off the window sill from where he had been spitting cherry stones at a puzzled squirrel helping itself to peanuts from the feeder hanging outside. He bounced up onto the bed. 'When does our adventure continue?'

Demelza grabbed Nessa's arm, which was dangling down from her bunk, and checked the time on her calculator watch. 'It's only twelve, so we could leave after lunch.'

'Lunch?' said the pickled knight in disgust. 'Lunch is for the weak. I haven't eaten lunch in a millennium!'

'Yeah, but you're gutless,' yawned Nessa, hanging over the edge of the bunk.

'Gutless? Why I'm the bravest, boldest— Oh, you mean I no longer have guts.'

'Bingo.' Nessa sat up and pulled on her denim jacket. 'Come on, we can't go grave hunting on empty stomachs.'

Demelza's dad hadn't had time to make lunch. He had spent the morning snoozing on the sofa after sitting up all the previous night with Captain Honkers. Instead, he gave Demelza some money to buy something to eat from Lamorna Bocaddon's café in town.

Demelza noticed Nessa peering through the window of Saffron Records on the way past to see if her idol, Karensa Polkerris, was working that day.

The café was quite busy considering there weren't many tourists on the island once summer was over.

'Hello, Mrs Bocaddon,' said Demelza as a woman wearing lots of make-up and huge earrings sat them down in the last booth.

'Hello, Demelza, and hello, Demelza's friend. And, as I keep telling your father, it's *Miss* Bocaddon.'

'I'm Nessa,' said Nessa, shaking her hand. 'I'm new to Penfurzy.'

'Oh, you're the family who bought the old windmill. How lovely to see it all painted and pretty again.' The café owner looked down at Captain Honkers who was pattering around under the table, snapping up the remnants of other people's meals. 'We don't usually allow pets in here, but your dad did say Honkers hasn't been well, so I'll make an exception this once.' She preened her hair in the mirror and gave a funny little smile as she asked, 'So, how is your dad, Demelza? Aren't you both lonely up there, just the two of you?'

'We're fine,' said Demelza, narrowing her eyes as she wondered if there was another reason *Miss* Bocaddon brought so many cakes and pies up to the house. 'We'll have fish finger sandwiches, fruit scones and two glasses of lemonade please.' She snapped the menu closed and handed it back before Miss Bocaddon could ask anything else.

Nessa seated her backpack carefully on the bench next to her, nudging away Captain Honkers who kept sticking his head inside to honk at the pickled knight who was nestled at the bottom next to the Pendragon Cup.

'I've been looking at this,' said Demelza. She pushed the theme-park map across the table and stabbed her figure down on the ride furthest from the entrance.'This is the highest point in Piskie Parc. I bet this ride was built on top of the barrow thing. That's where we have to take the cup.'

'Whiplash Whirligig?' said Nessa. 'That's like a roller coaster?'

'Kind of,' said Demelza. 'It goes underground for a bit. Mebbe we can follow the track and fixnd the entrance, although we need to be careful, cos I heard people have gone missing down there.

PISKIE
PARC

WHIRLIGIG
KINGDOM
SPACE
SPECTRE
LASER
KINGDOM

Derwa Crimp in my class said that her sister heard from her friend who heard from her cousin, Merrin Carnkie who used to work there, that the ride once went into the hill with ten people in it and came out empty.'

'Hmm, I think that might have made the news if it had happened,' said Nessa. She pulled a face as she pointed out an area of the map decorated with unicorns, fluffy pink kittens, fairies and princesses in big froofy pastel-coloured dresses with *far* too many ribbons. 'What's *that* bit?'

'Urgh. THAT is the Princess Pageant,' said Demelza as they tucked into their sandwiches. 'The rides go slower than you can walk and they play tinkly nursery rhymes.'

'Perfect for you, Smellza,' said a voice from the booth next to theirs. Demelza snarled as Connan Lenteglos's grinning head popped up over the back of the bench.

He stopped smiling as Demelza growled and leapt up to grab him by the black strings of the silver ram's-skull tie that he wore around his neck.

'Aargh, gerroff!' he squealed as she pulled it tight. She could hear Jory and Trevik laughing from the booth behind him. 'Chill out,' he spluttered as his face went red. 'I just wanted to ask about Honkers - the vet told my mum he's alive?'

'It's CAPTAIN Honkers,' said Demelza, letting go of his necktie before his head exploded. 'And yes, he's alive, no thanks to your stupid dog.' Right on cue, Captain Honkers flapped up onto the back of the bench and pecked Connan right on his shiny nose.

Connan shrieked and held his nose as Demelza pulled Captain Honkers away and kissed the top of his head.

'Ee ooks ine!' said Connan, staring at the goose.

'Of course he looks fine!' said Demelza. 'We went and got the magic Pendragon Cup an' saved him, an' now we're taking it back to—'

A loud coughing came from Nessa's backpack but was drowned out by a weird, very loud laugh from Nessa.

'HAHAHAA! Good one, D!' She slapped Demelza on the back. 'He looks like he believes you.'

Demelza bit her tongue as she realized how much she had said. She joined in with Nessa's false laugh. Connan looked from one to the other, then frowned and slipped back down into his booth. Demelza listened but couldn't hear what he was saying to his friends.

'Sorry,' she said to Nessa. 'My mouth went all blabby.'

'You need to be careful, D,' said Nessa as she spread cream on her scone and blobbed a spoonful of jam on the top. 'You were telling him everything!' She went to take a bite of the scone, then paused and looked around. The café had gone silent. Everyone was looking at them, mouths agape. Miss Bocaddon dropped the teapot she was holding. An old lady snarled. Even Captain Honkers had stopped hissing at Connan over the back of the booth and turned to watch Nessa, open-beaked. Nessa paused, scone half raised to her mouth.

'What's up?'

'Put the scone down and walk away,' Demelza whispered. She slid out of her seat and grinned nervously around the café as she grasped Nessa's arm.

'Sorry,' she said, backing towards the door and dragging Nessa with her. 'She's not from Penfurzy, she didn't know.' She held out her arms protectively as she backed away, shoving Nessa behind her. Captain Honkers raised his wings and hissed warningly as a man in a yellow anorak raised his arm to throw a bun at them. Demelza finally reached the door. She flung it open, sending the chimes jangling. 'Go-go-go!' she shouted to Nessa.

They darted outside and leapt on their bikes.

'Fly!' yelled Demelza. They cycled away at a million miles an hour, wind whipping through their hair, Demelza's anorak cape flapping behind her and Captain Honkers flying overhead honking for them to ride faster as they whizzed through the streets and finally left the town behind.

'We should be safe now,' panted Demelza as they reached the first sign for Piskie Parc. She pulled over to the side of the road and flopped over her handlebars. 'Pheeeew! That was close. We'd better not show our faces in there for a LONG time!'

'What in Honkers' name was that all about?' said Nessa as she hopped off Neon Justice and leant to one side to get rid of a stitch.

'Your scone,' said Demelza, eyes wide. 'You put the cream on first, THEN the jammy goodness.'

Nessa stared at her blankly. 'And?'

'And we never-ever-ever-ever, never-never-never-ever do that. On Penfurzy, jam goes first. AAAAALWAYS.'

Honk! said Captain Honkers in agreement.

'Penfurzy is bonkers,' said Nessa, getting back on her bike. 'But OK, in future – jam first.' Her backpack shook impatiently. Now that they were safely out of town, Nessa pulled out the pickled knight and popped him into her basket.

'About time,' he grumbled, spitting out an eraser and a flutter of pencil shavings.

'Soz, Pickles, nearly there. Let's get groovin'.'

They set off down the crumbling, mossy road, following the big, faded signs towards Piskie Parc. Nessa bellowed out the awful, cheesy slogans on each sign they passed:

'You should be a ringmaster!' Demelza laughed at Nessa's dramatic, booming voice.

'I was for a while,' sniffed Nessa. 'I ran off to join the circus when I was six. We went all over the world, but I had to quit cos I was allergic to clowns.'

Demelza nodded. Clowns were the worst.

Captain Honkers launched himself into the air and flew for a while, stretching his perfectly healed wings. A rumbling snore was coming from Nessa's basket.

Demelza chewed her lip as they cycled, then looked sideways at Nessa.

'You've done a lot of things before you came to Penfurzy. What about when you grow up? What do you want to be? A stunt pilot? A secret agent?'

Nessa shrugged as she skirted a pothole. 'I guess being a writer would be pretty cool. Creating characters and worlds for readers to explore in their heads.'

'You'd be good at that,' grinned Demelza. 'Making stuff up.'

'Watch it, Freckles,' said Nessa. 'So, what do you want to do?'

Demelza thought about it as they cycled through the fallen leaves. She hadn't really imagined anything beyond helping her dad at the caravan park and crazy golf course. What else could she do? She didn't ever want to leave Penfurzy, but maybe she'd have to when she grew up. She pushed the thought away and wished she hadn't started the conversation.

'You're a brilliant artist,' said Nessa at last. 'We should make comics together. I'll write the stories, you draw them.'

Demelza nodded. 'I'd like that. We could make comics about our adventures.'

'We'd better make them good ones then!' smiled Nessa as they rounded a corner. In front of them, a gigantic sign arched over the road:

'Tah-DAAAAAAAA!' sang Demelza.

They cycled down the empty car lanes towards the tollbooths, ducked under the barriers and whizzed up to the giant gates to the park. They were locked tight. A banner ran from one side to the other.

Closed for the Winter.

'Do you think you could pick that?' asked Demelza, running her hand over the rusty lock.

'Probably,' said Nessa. 'But why bother if we don't need to. There's always an easier way in. Come on.'

They followed the high, rickety wooden fence around the park. Every time they came to a big bush, Nessa ducked behind it then came back out shaking her head. Finally, from behind the biggest bush they had passed so far, Nessa let out a whoop.

'Found it! Come on in,' she shouted.

Demelza followed Captain Honkers as he waddled after Nessa. She squeezed her bike between the bush and fence to find Nessa wriggling through a big hole in the rotten fence. She pushed Neon Justice after her friend, then followed her through.

'There's always a way for kids to sneak into these places,' said Nessa, helping Demelza drag her bike through the bushes on the other side.

'Bravo, Trespasser!' cheered the pickled knight.

They brushed themselves down and stared around. The wind flapped the shutters on the closed snack stands, sent clouds of leaves swirling around the silent park and fluttered the sails of Skunkbeard's Swinging Ship of Doom which loomed to their left,.

'Where to?' asked Nessa.

Demelza pointed towards the other side of the park where a towering roller coaster stood cold and dark against the grey sky – a giant dinosaur skeleton standing guard over the hill beneath it.

'There it is,' said Demelza. 'The Great Barrow.'

YAAARGH!!
CAROUSEL
INFO
WRISTBA
FOR WINTER
WELCOM

Chapter Thirteen
ZIP-ZIP AND AWAAAAAY!

The park was eerily quiet as they cycled through its empty avenues and skirted around the pastel-coloured Tinkly Teacups, the Choo-Choo Hullaballoo and the Capering Carousel with its rearing horses, most of which were missing ears and tails.

'Watch this, D,' said Nessa, dismounting by a row of wooden cut-out figures. She went round the back and stuck her head through the head hole of a man in Bermuda shorts balanced on a surfboard and pretended to scream down at the badly painted shark biting the board. Demelza pulled her big plastic camera out of her bag, put the little viewfinder up to her eye and snapped a picture. A white square popped out of a slot at the front. Demelza pulled it out and wafted it gently until the picture of surf dude Nessa appeared.

'Awesome!' said Nessa, slipping the photo into her jacket pocket.

'Now do me!' Demelza stuck her head through a hole in a pram, a flowery baby bonnet above her head. She opened her mouth wide and wailed like a baby as Nessa took a picture.

'Now me!' the pickled knight hopped out of Nessa's basket as she wafted the picture into existence.

HONK! said Captain Honkers, following the pickled knight to the cut-outs.

'OK, wait for it!' Demelza balanced the camera on a bin and set a timer before hurrying to join the others. She climbed onto a step behind the stands and stuck her face through the head hole of a medieval knight, Captain Honkers flying up to perch on her helmet. Nessa became a ridiculously muscly man in a stripy vest holding a barbell up in the air with one hand. She scrunched up her face and puffed out her cheeks until they were bright red as if with the effort of holding up the weights. The pickled knight wriggled his head through a hole to become the strangest, ugliest little dog they had ever seen.

'One, two, three . . .' counted Demelza.

'YAAAAAAARG!' they all shouted as the camera clicked and whirred.

‘Sweet!’ said Nessa. She grabbed the photo and held it high. ‘The first official group picture of the new Penfurzy Rebel Bicycle Club.’

Demelza and Nessa did their special handshake but paused mid hip-bump as someone shouted in the distance: ‘Smellllllzaaaaaah! Nessieeeeee-Wessieeeeeee!’

‘Man, even his insults are lame,’ said Nessa as Connan’s annoying voice echoed through the empty park, followed by the hooting laughter of Jory and Trevik.

‘Gah. Me and my jabber-jaws! I can’t believe they followed us!’ Demelza jumped onto her bike. ‘Come on, let’s get to the barrow before they see us.’

‘Run? Never! Stay! Fight to the death!’ shouted the pickled knight, leaping out of Nessa’s basket and bouncing in the direction of the voices. ‘They shall witness our might! They shall cower before us!’

‘Whoa! Peace, little dude!’ said Nessa, cycling after him and sweeping him up like a rugby ball, his battle cries suddenly muffled by her armpit. ‘Fighting is for lame-os. Let’s just do what we came to do.’

Demelza could hear him muttering angrily into Nessa’s armpit as they cycled the neverending twisty-turny paths towards the

Whiplash Whirligig.

Honk. Hoooonk! Captain Honkers warned from the skies.

'Bum drops,' said Demelza, looking back over her shoulder. Connan and his friends, Jory and Trevik, were cycling around the Tipsy Tornado with General Barkley bounding after them. 'Quick, this way!' She veered to the left, past a sign for the Treetop Trial. A fence hid them from the boys' view as they zoomed towards a little wood at the edge of the park. Demelza pointed to a steep ramp that led up into the trees.

'Think you can make it up there?' she shouted to Nessa.

'Just watch me!' Nessa's legs became a blur as she put on a massive burst of speed in the run-up to the ramp.

'Go-go-go!' shouted Demelza. They hit the ramp at full speed, fighting against the stiffening pedals as the slope stole their speed. Finally, when the effort was too great, they jumped off their bikes and dragged them to the top of the ramp and into a treehouse that sat between two trees.

'Get down,' said Nessa. They flung their bikes to the floor and ducked down below the windows. Demelza wrapped her arms around Captain Honkers and pulled him to the floor with them just as General Barkley bounded into the wood, barking excitedly.

Trevik's voice carried up to them. 'Thought you said they went this way, Connan?'

Demelza and Nessa each found knotholes in the wood and peered down at the boys. General Barkley was trying to pee on as many trees as he could. The three boys were wheeling their bikes between the trees, searching.

'They did. You saw them too, didn't you, Jory?'

Jory shrugged. 'Looked like it. Mebbe they went that way.' He nodded towards the sparkly pink signs for the Princess Pageant.

Demelza made a face at Nessa and whispered, 'As IF!' Captain Honkers tried to wriggle out from under her arm, desperate to fly down and peck General Barkley's skinny waggy tail. 'Stop it, Honkers!' she hissed. 'I'm not letting you get hurt ever-ever-ever again.'

Nessa was having as much difficulty with the pickled knight. She gagged him with one of her sweatbands and held on tight as he tried to roll out of her arms and down the ramp like a bowling ball.

'I know you want to fight,' she whispered, 'but what are you going to do? Nibble their toes?'

'I think they're going,' said Demelza, eye pressed to the hole.

Jory and Trevik were cycling towards the Princess Pageant. Connan poked a stick into the last couple of bushes then called his dog.

'Barkley! Come on, this way, boy!'

'Uh-oh,' whispered Demelza as the dog ignored him and sniffed closer and closer. 'Get lost, doofus dog.' But General Barkley was following his nose right to the bottom of the ramp where he threw back his head and howled. Demelza's heart thudded.

'Jory! Trev! Get back here!' yelled Connan. 'They're in the trees. They can't get away - they must have taken their bikes with them!'

He dropped his bike and started up the ramp as the other two raced back. General Barkley chased his tail in excitement.

'Nooo! I thought they'd never look up here.' said Demelza. 'There's no way out!!'

Nessa pressed a button on the yellow siren on her handlebars. The boys jumped at the ear-splitting wail.

'Police!' shouted Jory as he began to run with Trevik.

'Of course it's not!' shouted Connan. 'It's coming from the treehouse!'

Captain Honkers wriggled free at last and swept down the ramp to peck at the heads of the boys as they rushed for the ramp. General Barkley barked up at the goose, wild with excitement.

'Aargh, ow! Gerrim off!' shouted Trevik, rubbing his head as Honkers whizzed past and snapped up a beak full of hair.

'Look, we just want that cup you got,' shouted Connan, ducking as the goose dive-bombed them again.

'What cup?' Demelza shouted back, hurling a handful of bangers down at Connan who leapt off the ramp as they exploded at his feet, sending General Barkley bonkers.

'You know what cup!' shouted Trevik, as Demelza rained down more bangers. 'We heard you talking about it, and the vet is telling everyone that you cured Honkers by pouring magic water over him from a weird cup. We know you were bringing it here, so hand it over!'

'CAPTAIN Honkers!' shouted Nessa through her bike microphone. She hurled a few bangers along with a handful of conkers. 'If you want the cup, you can try and take it!'

'What are you doing?' asked Demelza as the boys ducked the conkers and began dragging themselves up the steep ramp by the rope rail. 'There's no way out!'

‘What about that way?’ Nessa pointed at two zip-lines which led down from the other side of the treehouse.

‘We’d have to leave our bikes,’ said Demelza. ‘Even with the head start they’d catch us in no time on foot!’

‘Who said we’d be leaving our bikes?’ smiled Nessa, covering the pickled knight with her jacket and plonking him back into her basket. She wheeled her bike to the edge of the long drop down to the ground. ‘Watch and learn.’ She climbed onto the bike and reached up to grab the handgrips hanging from one of the zip-lines. Demelza realized what she was going to do. It was risky. Very risky. But she wasn’t going to let Connan get his hands on the cup. She wheeled her own bike over beside Nessa, climbed on and grabbed the handgrips above her head.

‘Are you sure this will work?’ she asked, trying not to look down to where a tiny General Barkley was yapping excitedly up at them.

Nessa shrugged. ‘No, but it’s worth a shot.’ She wrapped her legs through the frame of Neon Justice. ‘Ready?’

‘Nope,’ said Demelza, tying her own legs in knots to hold onto her bike. As Connan and Jory had reached the treehouse Nessa gave Demelza a nod.

'Wait!' yelled Connan, lurching forwards as Demelza and Nessa swung forwards at the same time. With a whizzing whoosh, they were off!

'WOOOOOOOOOOOOO!' screamed Nessa as the world fell away.

HONK!

honked Captain Honkers, launching himself after them.

'WAAAAAAAAAH!'

screamed Demelza, then

'WAAAAAAH-WAAAAA-HOOOOOOO!'

They were flying their bikes through the trees! Her stomach flipped over and over as her flying bike carried her to safety, like a metal Pegasus. The feeling was incredible.

A fence loomed below them.

'Up!' shouted Nessa. Demelza heaved her bike up with her legs and they cleared the fence.

'Aaaaand drop!' hollered Nessa as they whizzed towards the ground.

Demelza barely had time to think. She let go of the handgrips, grabbed her handlebars, unwrapped her legs from the bike frame and slammed her feet onto the pedals just as the back tyre hit the ground.

'Killer landing!' yelled Nessa, wheelieing along beside her and holding up her hand for a high five.

Demelza let out a whoop and slapped Nessa's palm, unable to believe what they had just done. She glanced back at the treehouse to see Connan, Trevik and Jory gaping down at them like bug-eyed goldfish. She stuck out her tongue, put her thumb to her nose and waggled her fingers triumphantly as they spurred their steeds on towards King Pendragon's tomb.

Chapter Fourteen
BLOOD FOR THE BLOOD GOD

The Whiplash Whirligig cast its skeletal shadow down over the park as the sun dropped lower in the autumn sky.

'Nearly there!' panted Demelza, slowing to pull out the park map and opening it across her handlebars, confident that Connan and friends were way behind after having to climb back down for their bikes. 'Just round this corner and straight through the gates of Castle-Crasher Kingdom and—Ohhhhhh.'

Her bike brakes squealed as the gates of the castle that marked the centre of the park came into view.

The portcullis was down.

There was no way through.

'No way I can pick that,' said Nessa, kicking one of the metal bars. 'What's plan B?'

Demelza's stomach went cold as she looked at the map. 'We could go left, but that's the long way round, and we'd run into the boys before we reached the tunnel. If we take the quick route to the right . . .'

'We'll still run into them,' said Nessa, following the trail with her finger.

Demelza slumped. 'Maybe we should just come back and try again tomorrow?' she sighed.

There was a cough from Nessa's basket. 'Perhaps I should have mentioned this sooner . . .' said the pickled knight, 'but it MUST be returned by sunset this evening or I will be forever cursed to roam this land as a blue bouncing bonce!'

'Gah,' shouted Demelza. 'Time limits! Why are there always time limits?'

'Remember what I told you?' said Nessa, punching her lightly on the arm. 'The BEST adventures have time limits. And . . . I have a PLAN. Come on, we're taking the short route.'

'But they'll catch us,' said Demelza, cycling after her.

'Nope, those boys couldn't catch a cold!' said Nessa, performing a bunny hop that made the pickled knight bounce up into the air.

Captain Honkers honked excitedly as he glided above them, perfect wings spread wide. Demelza could hardly believe it was the same goose who couldn't even lift his head from the kitchen table early that morning. If only they could keep the cup so that he could live for ever. She couldn't imagine him ever . . . She shoved the thought from her mind and sped after Nessa.

General Barkley's barks were getting louder now, followed by the shouts of Connan and his gang.

'Nearly there!' Nessa called over her shoulder.

Where? thought Demelza. Connan's gang was going to catch them and take the cup. What was Nessa thinking?

They reached a hulking dark entranceway. Nessa picked the padlock on the chain holding the ride doors closed and flung them open.

'Follow me!'

'But it's pitch-black in there!' Demelza called into the gaping mouth of the mysterious ride. But as General Barkley yapped excitedly and Captain Honkers honked warnings from above, she took a deep breath and rode inside.

Nessa used the chain to padlock the door behind them again and flicked a switch. The cavern they were in was filled with a strange dark blue light and the walls lit up with neon splashes, stars and glowing planets.

‘Space Spectre Laser Kingdom,’ breathed Demelza.

The sweatbands on Nessa’s wrists and the neon paint on her bike glowed brightly in the darkness, as did Demelza’s green and orange odd socks and the white zip of her anorak. Captain Honkers waddled around in circles, honking proudly at his glowing white feathers.

‘Witchcraft!’ gasped the pickled knight peering out from under Nessa’s jacket.

‘Nope. Black-lights,’ said Nessa. She placed her finger over her lips and cupped a hand behind her ear. Demelza held her breath and listened. General Barkley was right outside now, whining and scratching at the door. She squeaked and clamped a hand over her mouth as the door rattled, shaking the chains on the inside.

‘Get down, Barkers!’ shouted Connan as the dog barked outside the door. ‘They must have tried to hide in here, but couldn’t. It’s chained shut.’

‘They can’t be far, then,’ said Trevik. ‘Let’s go find ’em!’

‘Man, those guys are The Worst,’ said Nessa as the voices faded. ‘Grade A Lame-os.’

‘What now, fellow warriors?’ asked the pickled knight. ‘I could chase them from this strange kingdom and bring you their eyes?’

'Hold up, Headlong Harry,' said Nessa, catching the back of her jacket as it bounced away wrapped around the pickled knight. 'What would we do with their eyes? No. No chasing. We're cutting through the ride. Quietly! By the time we come out the other side we should have lost them.'

'Oh,' said the pickled knight as Nessa plonked him back into her basket. He sighed. 'This modern world just doesn't know how to do battle.'

'Oh, it does,' said Nessa. 'But the spit sisters? We're all about peace, bro.' She nodded to Demelza as she clipped her torch onto her shoulder. 'Stick close, D. We're going in!'

Demelza took a deep breath and wheeled her bike after Nessa into the creepy blue darkness, skirting around a glowing cut-out of a two-headed purple alien that loomed out of the shadows and dodging the papier-mâché space ghouls and goblins lurking around every corner. She was glad she was with Nessa - Space Spectre Laser Kingdom was not such a fun place to be when it wasn't full of laughing screaming kids with laser guns that went **pew-pew.**

WARP
ZONE

'Nessa, do you ever get scared?' she asked quietly.

'Sometimes,' said Nessa, glancing over her shoulder. 'Why?'

'Cos I think you're the bravest person I ever met. I don't think you get scared of anything.'

Nessa was quiet for a minute. The only sounds were the pattering of Captain Honkers' feet and the gentle clicking of their bike wheels. 'You know what really scares me?' she said at last. 'More than anything?'

Demelza gulped. 'What? Spider nests in your bed? Maggots in your sandwiches? Giant nits? Piranhas coming up out of the bath plughole?'

Nessa leant back and gave Demelza's arm a light punch. 'No, daft nut! The thought of not having a best friend like you.'

'Oh.' Demelza flushed deep red as she smiled in the darkness. 'Well, you don't ever need to be scared about that.'

Nessa grinned at her. 'Although now all can think about is giant nits. Thanks for that, D.'

'You were pretty a-feared when you saw me atop the caravan,' mumbled the pickled knight from under the jacket in Nessa's basket.

'Shh!' said Demelza. 'Here's the exit.' She put a finger on Honkers' beak to tell him to stay quiet as they put their ears to the door. They could hear dry leaves rustling as the wind swept them past the bottom of the door.

'OK,' said Nessa. 'They're gone. Let's roll.' She pushed open the door and they blinked in the light as they wheeled their bikes outside. The sun was glaring low in the sky, casting long shadows across the park as they began to ride off.

'We'd better be quick,' said Demelza. 'Not long 'til sunset.'

'Aww, you ickle girlies scared of the dark?' said Jory, popping up from behind a bush.

Demelza screeched her bike to a halt as Connan and Trevik popped up too, grinning.

'Yeah, sure,' said Nessa. 'We took a detour through the super-dark Laser Kingdom because we're scared of the dark. Got to admit, I thought you'd be too dumb to realize we were in there.'

'Thanks to Barkers!' said Connan proudly as his dog bounced around them, woofing at Captain Honkers who was perched on a hot dog stand hissing down at him. 'The General lost track of your stink out here, so we knew you were still hiding.'

'Oooh, Sherlock Holmes!' said Demelza, rolling her eyes.

'Come on, Connan, just leave us alone. We've got stuff to do.'

'The only stuff you've got to do is to give us that cup,' said Jory, rolling up his sleeves.'

'Oh wow, he rolled up his sleeves,' said Nessa, biting all of her fingernails. 'I guess we *have* to give it to them now.'

Demelza could see Nessa's jacket begin to shake in her basket as the pickled knight beneath fought the urge to do battle. An idea tickled her brain. She slumped down in her seat and made her voice all quiet and squeaky,

'N . . . Nessa, muh . . . maybe we should give them the cup? They're not going to leave us alone until we do.'

Nessa's jaw almost dropped right off. She turned to stare at Demelza, hand on her jacket to stop it hopping out of the basket as the pickled knight quaked with rage.

'Sorry, Nessa.' Demelza hung her head as she walked her bike closer. 'They beat us. Let's just give it to them and go.'

'That's the first clever thing I've heard you say, Smellza,' said Connan. 'Come on then, hand it over.'

Demelza peeked up at Nessa as she pulled alongside her. Nessa had raised one of her eyebrows. 'What are you up to, D?' she murmured out of the corner of her mouth.

'What was that?' asked Connan.

'Nothing.' Demelza lifted Nessa's jacket out of the basket and held it out to Connan. 'Well? Do you want the cup or not?'

'Bit big, isn't it?' said Trevik.

'Yup,' said Nessa. 'Heavy too. It's made of gold.'

'Goooold!' said all three boys as they leant towards the jacket. Connan held General Barkley by the collar as the dog sniffed and whined longingly at the interesting whiff drifting from under the jacket.

'Why don't you uncover it?' asked Connan, narrowing his eyes.

'It loses some of its magic when it's touched by human hands,' said Demelza quickly.

'Who cares when it's made of gold!' said Jory, lunging for it.

'Hold on, Trev.' Connan pulled him back. 'Maybe we can make more money getting people to pay us to heal them with it.

'Perhaps you could heal yourselves first,' said Nessa. 'Cos that's just sick, and not in a good way.'

'Do you want it, or not?' Demelza walked her bike forward a couple of steps.

'Whoa, back up,' said Connan. 'I'll send the General over for it. Go on, Barkers, get the cup.' He let go of the dog's collar and General Barkley bounded forwards, snatched the jacket from Demelza's grasp and shook it around in its jaws.

'Bad Barkers.' Connan slapped his palms loudly on his thighs. 'Come on, bring it here, boy. Bring us the cup.'

The dog paused as though wondering whether to make this into a fun game, but his master didn't look in the mood for chasing. He pattered over to Connan and gave up the jacket with just a little tussle and a slight growl.

'OK, you've got the cup,' said Nessa, rubbing her bare arms. 'Now can I have my jacket back?'

'Fair enough,' said Connan. 'Trev, gimme your scarf to wrap the cup in.'

'Why my scarf?' said Trevik. 'I'll get a cold if I don't wear it. Use Jory's hat.'

'No way,' said Jory. 'You know I get earache.'

'Gah, you're giving me earache!' Connan whipped off his blue body warmer ready for the cup, then began to unbutton the bulging denim jacket. General Barkley wove in and out between the bikes, whimpering with excitement. Demelza and Nessa held their breath, glancing at the setting sun. The jacket was awfully still. Demelza worried that the pickled knight had already—

'RAAAARRRGH! YOUR SOULS ARE OURS!' roared the pickled knight, launching himself from the jacket so fast he ricocheted from Connan's forehead and into Jory, who he bit on the nose before bouncing off the side of Trevik's head, knocking all three boys and bikes over like dominoes.

'EEEEEeeeeEEEEeeEE!' shrieked Connan in such a high pitch that General Barkley started howling.

'WaaaaaAAAAAaaaH!' wailed Jory.

'GED-IT-AWAY, GED-IT-AWAY, GED-IT-AWAY, pleeeeeaaase!' squealed Trevik, trying to wriggle away backwards into a bush as the pickled head bounced towards his face, snapping its yellow teeth.

'Z . . . z . . .' squeaked Connan as he leapt on his bike. 'It's a z . . . z . . .'

The pickled knight hopped towards him, cackling. 'The word you are looking for . . .' he said as he took a huge leap up onto Connan's shoulder and hissed in his ear, 'is zombieeee.'

'AAAAIIIIeeeeeeeeeEEEEEE!'

With a clatter of bikes the boys shot from the clearing so fast their shadows took seconds to catch up. General Barkley snapped at the pickled knight as he tumbled from Connan's shoulder, but the knight was too quick. He grasped the dog's collar with his teeth and spurred his ride after the boys, whooping and yelling muffled war cries from his howling mongrel steed.

'Fear our fury! We shall feast on your flesh! Blood for the Blood God! Teeth for the er . . . TOOTH FAIRY!'

‘Genius,’ gasped Nessa, holding her sides to stop herself exploding with laughter. ‘You’re a genius, D.’

‘Hoooo, hoooo!’ gasped Demelza, unable to say anything for the tears pouring down her cheeks as they watched the pickled knight riding after the boys, their screams filling the empty park. ‘Hoooo, hoooo!’

Hooonk! Hoooonk! said Captain Honkers, landing between them and flapping his wings in applause as the pickled knight circled back and rode victoriously towards them.

‘Bravo!’ shouted Demelza, catching the head as the knight’s head leapt from General Barkley’s back.

‘All hail Sir Calenick!’ shouted Demelza, holding his head high. Nessa saluted the knight as General Barkley ran yapping after the boys, tail tucked between his legs.

Chapter Fifteen
THE GUARDIAN

The setting sun winked through the roller coaster's metal frame as Nessa and Demelza rode full pelt towards the Whiplash Whirligig.

'This way!' Demelza veered to the left and followed the tracks, screeching to a halt where the tracks disappeared into a tunnel that led down through the hill. 'That's the way in.'

They left their bikes leaning against the fence as they pulled on their backpacks. She pulled on her head torch and Nessa switched on the torch under the shoulder strap of her jacket.

'The dead need no light!' said the pickled knight as Nessa offered him the spare head torch. He hopped on into the gaping tunnel. 'Come. I sense something within this barrow. It's expecting us. Let's not keep it waiting.'

'Um, what exactly is down here?' said Demelza as they followed the pickled knight down into the barrow. 'I really don't mind keeping it waiting.'

The pickled knight bounced on in silence, following the maintenance path that wound down into the darkness alongside the tracks. The torches caused strange shadows to bob around them as they descended into the earth. Captain Honkers let out an excited honk as he found an extra-juicy, crunchy beetle, then pattered quickly after Demelza as his honks echoed back through the tunnel in a strange bouncy way.

Demelza linked arms with Nessa as the track dropped sharply and the ramp became a long flight of steps. It really did feel as though the hill was aware they were there and was watching them. Waiting for them.

'We come in peace,' she whispered, hoping it could tell they were bringing something back, rather than plotting to steal from the tomb.

Nessa squeezed her arm. 'Nearly there. We'll be back in your caravan playing *Legend of Melder* and eating all those Halloween sweets in no time.'

Demelza hoped she was right, but wished she had let her dad know where they were going. Would Connan, Jory and Trevik tell anyone where they were if they didn't come back? That was, if the boys hadn't all died of fright themselves.

The pickled knight stopped at the point where the tracks sloped back up towards the surface.

'We're close,' he said. 'The entrance to the barrow is around here somewhere. Imp, take out the cup.'

'Stop calling me— Oh, never mind!' sighed Demelza. She pulled the cup from her backpack and almost dropped it as its glow lit up the darkness. 'Why is it doing that?'

'It's showing us the way,' said the pickled knight. 'Follow it.'

'What do you mean?' asked Demelza. She walked forwards holding out the cup. 'Ohhhh!' The cup glowed brighter as she walked, then grew dim. She backed up and at the point where it had glowed brightest she noticed a little passage which led off from the path.

Captain Honkers pattered ahead as they squeezed down the little passage. The cup continued to glow, then hummed gently as they came to a dead end. Demelza ran her hand over the stone slab that blocked their path. It was covered with strange symbols.

The pickled knight bounced closer as Demelza held up the cup to light the slab. 'I seem to remember we need to make an offering to get in. Some water poured from the cup should do the trick.'

'We don't have any water!' said Demelza.

'I could go and fill the cup from the Whizzy Watersplash ride at the other end of the park,' said Nessa.

'No time,' said the pickled knight. 'Sunset is upon us. Blood would be an acceptable alternative. I'd offer, but I'm, er, a bit congealed at the moment.'

Captain Honkers waddled quickly behind Demelza's legs as the pickled knight hopped a little closer.

'Wait!' Demelza dived into her backpack and pulled out a bottle of cherryade. 'It's flat, so it's a bit like water, and it's red, like blood.' She twisted the cap and it opened with a sad little ***pffffht.***

'I very much doubt that will work,' said the pickled knight as Demelza filled the cup with the sugary drink and threw it over the stone.

Honk! said Captain Honkers. The symbols on the stone were lighting up, one by one, as the sticky red liquid ran into them. There was a grinding noise and a shower of dry soil rained down on them as the stone rolled aside, letting out a waft of musty ancient air from a small chamber beyond.

'I . . . well, I stand corrected,' said the pickled knight, hopping through into the chamber.

'Maybe one of us should stay outside?' said Nessa as they followed the knight. 'Just in case . . .' There was a boom as the stone rolled back into place behind them. 'Oh. OK. Never mind. Carry on!'

They shone their torches around the chamber. There wasn't much in there. Ancient tree roots ran down the walls and over a few rocks carved with swirling Celtic symbols.

'It's . . . not quite how I remember it,' said the pickled knight. 'I'm sure it was bigger, and I definitely remember a throne. Maybe this is the wrong—'

'Aargh! Something's got me!' shouted Nessa, clutching her ankle.

'SNAAAAAKES!' yelled Demelza, trying to tug the long brown creature off Nessa as it twisted around her leg. She had only held one snake before, but it had felt very smooth, despite the scales. This was hard and scratchy and didn't have scales. It wasn't a snake - it was . . . **'ROOOOOOTS!'** Tree roots were slithering out of the walls and across the floor towards them like cobras ready to strike. Demelza danced around as they tried to grab her legs, stomping any that got too close.

'There are too many!' roared Nessa, fighting to pull her foot free. Demelza lurched forward to help her, but was dragged back as a root snaked around her waist. She flailed around trying to free herself, but it held on tight. She tried digging her heels into the ground, but it was no use. She was dragged backwards towards the wall of the chamber alongside Nessa who was struggling furiously against the roots holding her firmly by the wrists and ankles.

HONK-HONNNK! Captain Honkers leapt onto the pickled knight's head, flapping his wings and snapping his beak at the roots reaching out for them as the knight bounced around the chamber screaming insults that Demelza didn't quite understand, but which left the air sizzling.

'Get away from my goose!' yelled Demelza, struggling to break free from the roots pinning her to the wall.

'Keep going, Pickles!' yelled Nessa. 'Don't let them catch you!'

'Yeeeargh!' screamed the pickled knight as he launched himself into the air and grabbed the closest root with his teeth. He bit down hard on the squirming tendril, growling like a dog. Captain Honkers honked encouragement at the top of his lungs.

HONK-HONK-HOOOOOOOONK!

'SILENCE!' boomed a voice. The roots stopped slithering. The pickled knight and Captain Honkers dropped to the floor. Demelza squeaked as a mass of roots on the opposite side of the chamber parted and two green hands with long pointed fingers reached out. The hands were followed by a snarling, wrinkled face with two glimmering eyes and wild matted hair.

'INTRUDERS!' it screamed.

'SPRIGGAN!' shouted the pickled knight, bouncing over to join Demelza and Nessa.

'Spriggan!' yelled Demelza. 'They're *real?*'

'What the Mordor is a spriggan?' asked Nessa, struggling to escape as the creature pulled itself out into the chamber, stretched its skinny arms wide and grew until its oversized head touched the ceiling.

'They're related to piskies. Remember, I showed you Mum's notebook about them,' said Demelza.

'Yeah, but piskies are nice, aren't they?'

'Mostly,' said Demelza, 'but spriggans are very, very not nice.'

Captain Honkers was used to chasing humans and animals many times his size and wasn't going to be intimidated by a spriggan. He spread his wings and gave the towering creature his loudest, most ferocious hiss. The spriggan bent down to the goose and spread its lips in a hideous grin to reveal an endless row of pointed brown teeth, then let out a hiss so long and loud Captain Honkers had to brace himself against the spit-filled hurricane. As the gale finally stopped, Captain Honkers paused, spun on one foot, pit-pattered over to Demelza and ducked down behind the pickled knight, tucking his head under his wing. The spriggan sniffed the air.

'Humans,' it spat. 'Noisy dirty humans with your rumbling trains and whooping and screaming. Now you come to raid the Great Barrow?'

'No, we're not here to— Mmphf!' Demelza was cut short as a root wrapped itself over her mouth.

'Rude!' said Nessa. 'She was trying to tell you— Mrrrmmphf!' Her eyes burned with rage as a root clamped over her mouth too.

Demelza's legs shook. She wondered if this was what had happened to the people who Derwa Crimp's sister's friend's cousin said had gone missing on the ride.

'Er, nice place,' said the pickled knight, grinning nervously up at the spriggan's gigantic head as it pondered what to do with them. 'Very homely. Been here long?'

'Home? Pah!' said the spriggan. 'My home was the cairn on top of the tor. Fresh air, a view of the whole island, but I left for just one day a few weeks ago, and on my return it was destroyed! A thousand-year-old cairn, gone!'

Demelza didn't think spriggans could read minds, but she made her eyes look as sympathetic as possible as she tried very hard not to think about how she had dismantled that very cairn with Nessa to find clues leading to the lost Penfurzy treasure.

'This barrow was empty, abandoned by the other spriggans when that metal monster was built on top of it. Winter should have brought peace and quiet, but no. It brought . . . YOU.'

Demelza gulped as the spriggan thrust its head towards them and grinned a terrible grin.

'So, which of you wants to be torn limb from limb first?'

'I'm a little short on limbs right now,' said the pickled knight, rolling back into Captain Honkers.

'Mmmmmmm! MMMMMM!' Demelza screamed into the root over her mouth, waving her hands and legs towards her fallen backpack as the root around her waist tightened. Nessa joined in, nodding towards the backpack as they both screamed;

'Mmmmmmm!

Mmmmmm-mmmm MMMMMMMMMPH!'

The spriggan winced and slapped its hands over its giant ears. 'Whaaaat?' it roared at last.

The roots around their mouths dropped away and Demelza yelled, 'We're not thieves! Look in my bag!'

The spriggan opened the backpack. A bright green glow lit up its wrinkled face as it reached inside and pulled out the wooden cup, lighting the entire cavern.

'The lost Pendragon Cup!' it gasped. Its other hand shot out and grabbed Demelza. It tore her from the grip of the roots and dangled her by the feet over its foul-smelling mouth. 'Explain!' it hissed up at her.

Chapter Sixteen
THE GREAT BARROW

Demelza held her breath at the stench and shivered as she stared down into the spriggan's jaws.

'Child. You have five seconds to tell me how you came to possess the most important treasure in all the land.'

'I . . . it was, well, we . . .' she stammered as she tried to explain without revealing that the pickled knight had pinched it.

The spriggan snapped its jaws and lowered her towards its needle-like teeth.

'Get off her!' yelled Nessa. Tearing one arm free, she grabbed her torch from her shoulder strap and hurled it at the spriggan. The creature howled as the torch smashed into its teeth then tumbled down its throat. It dropped Demelza and the cup and staggered around the cavern wheezing and clutching its neck as torchlight flashed out of its mouth. The roots holding Nessa dropped away as the spriggan fell to the floor.

'It's choking!' said Demelza as its arms and legs thrashed, its face turning from green to red to purple.

'Good, then let's get this back where it belongs!' said the pickled knight, grabbing the stem of the cup in his teeth and bouncing away from the spriggan's flailing legs.

'Wait!' shouted Demelza. 'We've got to help it!'

'Why?' said the pickled knight, dropping the cup in surprise. 'It tried to eat you!'

'We did break into its home,' said Nessa, rubbing her wrists, 'and it sounds as though we're the reason it's living down here now.'

Honk! said Captain Honkers.

'You too?' said the pickled knight, shaking his head and looking at the spriggan who was lying quite still, letting out little wheezing noises. The torch shone out of its mouth, lighting the ceiling.

‘OK, what’s the plan?’

‘Heimlich manoever!’ said Demelza, we saw a video on it at school. Hit him between the shoulders, if that doesn’t work we need to reach around from behind and give five sharp tugs, her,’ she clasped her hands in the centre of her torso under her ribs.

‘OK, let’s sit him up,’ said Nessa, taking one of his arms. Demelza took the other and they pulled and tugged with all their might, but it was no use, his gigantic head was way too heavy.

“Ugh, only one thing for it,’ said Nessa. ‘I’m going in!’ She rolled up her right sleeve, marched over to the spriggan and thrust her arm down its throat, right up to the armpit.

‘Urgh, someone needs a breath mint,’ she gasped as she fished around, grimacing with disgust at the slimy tongue as she avoided the vicious-looking teeth.

‘Got it, heads up!’ She tugged until the torch went flying out of the creature’s mouth and landed with a crunch and a splat in front of the pickled knight.

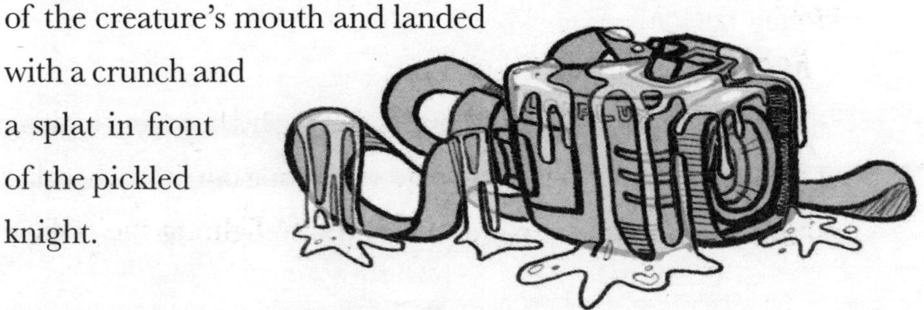

He leant sideways into Captain Honkers to wipe the spriggan spit from his cheek.

Demelza crept forwards. The spriggan had stopped wheezing, but its bony chest was barely moving.

'The cup!' Nessa held out her hand.

'Of course!' Demelza pulled out the bottle of cherryade and poured the tiny amount at the bottom of the bottle into the cup. 'Is that enough?'

'Let's see.' Nessa held the cup over the spriggan's mouth and let the cherryade trickle down its throat.

They waited. Captain Honkers pattered over and stared down into the spriggan's gaping mouth. **Honk!** he honked, then flapped away as his honks bounced around the smelly, toothy cave.

'Gnnngh,' said the spriggan. Its chest glowed as the green returned to his cheeks, sending Captain Honkers scurrying behind Demelza to peer over her shoulder as the creature shrank back to a size closer to human.

'Easy now,' said Nessa as the spriggan heaved itself into a sitting position. Its giant head wobbled as it looked around as if surprised to see them there.

'You . . . saved me?' It looked from Demelza to Nessa. 'Why?'

Nessa shrugged. 'Cos you needed saving.'

'But don't let it go to your head,' giggled the pickled knight.

'Dude!' said Nessa, pushing the bouncing head away. 'Not cool, especially from you!' They helped the spriggan to its feet.

'Thank you,' said the spriggan, as if it was the first time he had ever said those words. 'But you understand that I cannot let you leave this place with the lost Pendragon Cup? It is one of the treasures we spriggans are sworn to protect.'

'We're not leaving with it,' said Nessa.

'That's what we were *tryyyying* to tell you,' said Demelza, holding out the cup. 'Sir Pickles . . .'

'SIR CALENICK!' shouted the pickled knight.

'Sorry, Sir *Candlestick* found it an' we're just helping him bring it back.'

'You're not tomb raiders?' The spriggan scratched its huge head.

'No way,' said Demelza. 'We're tomb, er, returners!'

'Catchy,' said Nessa.

'So, Mr Spriggan,' Demelza offered it the cup again, 'if you'll just take it, we'll be off.'

The spriggan held up its palms and pushed the cup back. 'The borders are still thin after All Hallow's Eve - you should return it to him yourselves.'

'Him?' said Demelza.

'King Pendragon,' said the spriggan. It waved its hands at The gap he had crawled through into the chamber. The roots pulled back further revealing a small tunnel. I merely guard the entrance - his tomb is through there.

'Through that dark creepy tunnel right there?' said Demelza, chewing her thumbnail. 'There definitely isn't a door, or a light switch?' The spriggan turned and walked away, merging into a mass of roots without so much as a goodbye.

'Guess that's a no,' said Nessa. She stuck her head into the tunnel. 'Come on, let's get this over with so that Pickles can go home.'

Demelza squeezed into the tunnel behind Nessa and they crawled and wriggled their way through the roots, closely followed by the pickled knight and Captain Honkers. The tunnel was longer than Demelza expected and led deeper into the hill. The air was cold, earthy and damp. She shivered as they finally slipped out into another chamber. They couldn't see much, even in the light of the cup and torch, but judging from the echo this one was much bigger than the last.

'The Great Barrow,' said the pickled knight, bouncing around the room. 'Yes, I remember this! There's a throne over there, and a big slab with a fancy cloth over it somewhere around . . .'

'Here!' said a deep voice right next to them.

Demelza shone her torch in the direction of the voice to reveal a beautifully embroidered cloth lying over a stone slab. There was something shaped suspiciously like a body underneath it. Demelza braced herself for it to sit up and throw aside the cloth, revealing a maggoty corpse, so she was very surprised when it fell away to reveal a tall, very un-maggoty man with neat flowing hair and a beard. He sat up and smiled at them.

She fought the urge to drop to her knees as she stared up at his crown and the long robes he wore over his chain mail. He flicked his wrist and hundreds of candles sprang to life, lighting the huge chamber.

'Whoa!' said Nessa as the flickering light revealed that the curved tomb wall was adorned with tapestries of great battles. Celtic patterns swirled over the stone floor and up the painted stone pillars which held up the high arched ceiling. A chest overflowing with golden treasures sat on a raised platform in front of a throne which held a sword and a shield, but the most striking thing in the tomb was a huge round table at its centre. It was inlaid with different coloured woods in the shape of shields, each bearing a different symbol or creature. 'Sweet pad, dude!'

'Thank you,' said the king with a nod. 'If the spriggan let you through, I can assume you are not here to raid my tomb?'

'No, Mr Pendragon, sir,' said Demelza. 'We're helping our friend, Sir Calenick, bring something back.'

The king looked down as the pickled knight bounced forwards. 'Sir Calenick? You were not one of my knights?'

'No, my king. I am one of the Penfurzy knights who lived long after your reign. I have come to realize we were not as noble as your band of brothers.' He looked down at the floor. 'I'm the one who stole your cup.'

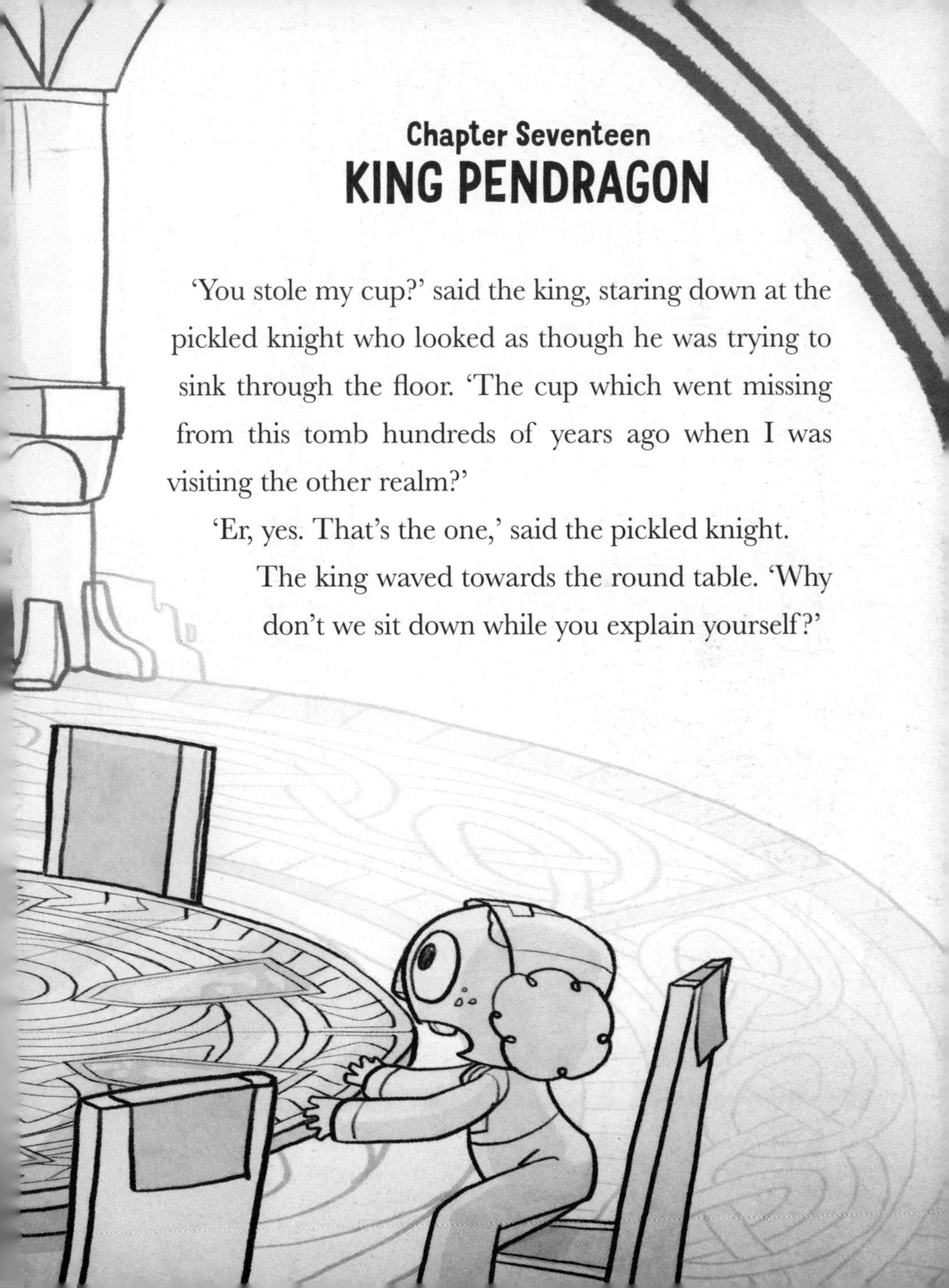

Chapter Seventeen
KING PENDRAGON

'You stole my cup?' said the king, staring down at the pickled knight who looked as though he was trying to sink through the floor. 'The cup which went missing from this tomb hundreds of years ago when I was visiting the other realm?'

'Er, yes. That's the one,' said the pickled knight.

The king waved towards the round table. 'Why don't we sit down while you explain yourself?'

Demelza and Nessa sat down and popped the pickled knight onto the ornate tabletop.

The king rested his chin on his fist and raised an eyebrow as the pickled knight shared how he had broken into the tomb and taken the cup, then found it to have strange powers.

'And when you realized this, you didn't think to return it?'

The pickled knight shifted uncomfortably on his stump. 'Well, it was a bit difficult. My brothers and I found—'

'Looted!' interrupted Nessa.

The pickled knight gritted his teeth at her, then sighed. 'OK, looted some cursed treasure overseas, killed each other, then found our souls trapped for ever in the castle we built to protect it. Trapped until the Imp and the Trespasser here found their way into our prison, broke the curse and returned the treasure.'

'So now we're helping him return the cup before sunset so that he can, er, you know . . .' Demelza drew a finger across her neck and let her tongue hang out.

'Kark it properly and go on to whatever comes next,' said Nessa.

Honk! added Captain Honkers, aware he hadn't said anything for a while.

Demelza pulled out the cup and turned to the pickled knight. 'You have been a loyal member of the Penfurzy Rebel Bicycle Club. We're sorry to lose you, Pickles, aren't we, Nessa?'

'It's been a blast, Calenick,' said Nessa, nodding to him. 'Wherever you're going, I hope you're happy there.'

Demelza pushed the cup into the king's hands and waited for something interesting to happen. Nothing remotely interesting happened.

The pickled knight looked awkward. 'I thank you for your help, brave Demelza and Nessa, but the sun set before we even entered the first chamber.

Demelza's face dropped as she looked at Nessa. 'We didn't make it in time!'

'We failed.' Nessa shook her head slowly. 'It was all for nothing. We failed in our quest.'

'Fail? How could you have failed?' said the pickled knight. 'You saved your goose, spoke with the Lady of the Lake, retrieved the cup, found the Great Barrow, fought your way in with bravery and cunning, saved the life of a spriggan who was about to extinguish yours and returned the great cup to King Pendragon. That does not sound like a quest failed!'

'But you're trapped here. Trapped for ever!' wailed Demelza, throwing her arms in the air. 'Without a body of your own. Just a head. A sad old mouldy head, bouncing around Penfurzy for ALL ETERNITY! Rotting away, all lonely and sad. Doooooomed to—'

'Cool it, D,' whispered Nessa, kicking her under the table. 'He gets it!'

'Oh, right!' Demelza giggled nervously as she sat back down and patted the pickled knight's hair. 'Of course you'll always be a member of the Penfurzy Rebel Bicycle Club.'

'An honour indeed,' said the pickled knight, bowing to them.

The king scratched behind his ear. 'You know, I know a few people. And you have learnt your lesson a thousandfold over the centuries, brave knight, and proven your worthiness in this quest. I'm sure if I put in a word you'd be able to move on.'

'Really?' said Demelza, jumping up and hugging the king around the waist. 'He can leave Penfurzy?' The thought suddenly made her feel a little sad.

'Leave Penfurzy?' said the knight, looking down at the patterns on the table.

'What's up?' asked Nessa. 'I thought you'd be dying to, er, die properly?'

The pickled knight did his shoulderless shrug. 'It's just that, these past few days . . . well, for the first time in centuries I've been having fun. I guess I was hoping to have a little more before passing on.'

'You want to stay?' said Demelza.

'I wouldn't mind having another adventure or two before I go.'

'Is that possible?' asked Nessa.

'You may leave this realm any time you like,' said the king.

Demelza clapped her hands, 'You can stay in one of the empty caravans and we'll all go adventuring every weekend!'

Honk! said Captain Honkers, rubbing his beak affectionately through the pickled knight's hair and snaffling up a beetle that was hiding in it.

There was a ringing sound as the king unsheathed the great shining sword at his waist. His face had turned serious. 'After hearing your story, there is something I must do now. Kneel!' he commanded.

Demelza and Nessa looked at each other.

'Why?' asked Nessa as the king ran a corner of his robe over the shining blade.

'When a king commands you to kneel, you kneel,'
said the king.

'Not us,' said Nessa. 'We kneel to no one. Especially not someone commanding us to.'

'Just do it,' hissed the pickled knight, bouncing into them to nudge them forwards.

'Forgive me,' said the king, bowing to them. 'Please, take a knee.'

Demelza thought he had asked very nicely, so she knelt down. Nessa grudgingly knelt beside her.

'Sir Calenick's tales show your bravery is great,' said the king. 'Such valour must be rewarded.'

'Like with some of that treasure?' asked Demelza, looking over to the chest overflowing with gold.

The king laughed. 'You could try to take it, but with a spriggan guarding the exit your life of riches would be short indeed.'

'Yeah yeah, questers never get to keep the treasure,' sighed Demelza.

'But I shall bestow upon you something I hope you will find greater than riches.' Demelza felt something tap her shoulder. She looked up to see the king's sword pass over her head to rest briefly on the other shoulder.

'Arise, Sir Demelza, Penfurzy Knight,' he announced. Demelza opened her mouth but no words came out.

The king touched the sword to Nessa's shoulders too. 'Arise, Sir Nessa, Penfurzy Knight.'

'OK, *maaaybe* that was worth kneeling for!' said Nessa as she spat on her hand and started the club handshake, ending with a big squeezy hug that Captain Honkers demanded to be a part of.

'I've, er, never knighted a goose before,' said the king, 'but I guess I could . . .'

'No need,' said Demelza. 'He's already a captain.'

The king nodded and sheathed his sword as the newest knights of the Penfurzy Table picked up their backpacks and prepared to leave.

'Before we go,' said Demelza, 'I have an idea I want to test out.' She handed King Pendragon the empty cherryade bottle. 'Please could we have some water from your cup?'

'What's that for?' asked the pickled knight as they waved goodbye to the king and squeezed back through the tunnel to the spriggan's chamber.

'You'll see.' Demelza smiled.

Penfurzy Trumpet

THOUSAND YEAR-OLD SKELETON GOES WALKABOUT

BY JACKSON LOVEGROVE

Chapter Eighteen
MR CALENICK

Thousand-year-old skeleton goes walkabout!

'Listen to this!' Demelza's dad sat back in his kitchen chair to read from the front cover of the *Penfurzy Trumpet* as Captain Honkers pecked at his breakfast. Demelza and Nessa grinned at each other over their saffron buns.

'Staff at the Penfurzy Museum were astounded to find the bones of a headless Penfurzy knight, found on top of the castle tower, have disappeared overnight. Merrin Carnkie, museum caretaker, told this reporter that several hours after closing time, the bones developed a strange green glow and grew a layer of skin before climbing out of the glass case and walking right past her, out of the museum and off up Penfurzy high street. But bear in mind that this is the same Merrin Carnkie who told us that there's a ghost train that runs from the quarry to Penfurzy docks every Halloween, that the Whiplash Whirligig in Piskie Parc is haunted, and that she saw a spriggan screaming on top of Penfurzy Tor a few weeks ago.

'Incidentally, earlier that day two girls accidentally spilled a whole bottle of water over the bones. It's this reporter's view that a surprise shower would be the last straw for any skeleton after having his bare bones ogled all day. I hope Sir Boneybits has found himself a more peaceful place to rest.'

'Sir Boneybits!' snorted Nessa. 'I'll have to tell him that one.'

'Two girls . . . ?' Demelza's dad looked over the top of the paper, one eyebrow raised. 'Didn't you two visit the museum yesterday?'

'Did we?' said Demelza, scratching her chin. 'We did sooo much yesterday, I can't remember.'

'Hmmm,' said her dad. The doorbell rang. He checked his watch, folded up the paper and put on his jacket. 'Try to remember to wash the dishes when you're done with breakfast. I'm off to interview someone who applied to help me out around the caravan park and golf course. He knows *a lot* about the Penfurzy knights. I wonder if I could get him to dress up and pretend to be one? The tourists would love that!'

Demelza shoved a whole cheese scone into her mouth to stop herself laughing as her dad opened the door to a tall man with a very familiar head. He appeared to be wearing quite a bit of make-up to cover the blue hue.

Honk-honk! Captain Honkers ran over to greet him and pattered around his feet, honking noisily.

'Mr Calenick, was it?' said Demelza's dad, shaking his hand. 'Well, Captain Honkers certainly seems to have taken a shine to you. Come on, I'll show you around.'

As Demelza's dad strode outside, followed by Captain Honkers, the pickled knight leant through the doorway and winked at Demelza and Nessa as he raised his whole head off his shoulders, as though tipping his cap. They waved frantically for him to pop it back on his shoulders before Demelza's dad saw.

'What do you fancy doing today, Sir Nessa?'

asked Demelza as she watched her dad giving the pickled knight the grand tour through the kitchen window. 'Another quest?'

Nessa swigged her juice and grabbed her bag. 'Well, we've got a cairn to rebuild for a spriggan and a pile of notebooks full of mysteries to read, but first things first, let's go buy Mr Calenick a scarf. He needs something to keep his head from dropping off!'

The sun was just starting to melt the white frost on the grass as they cycled out of the caravan park. They took their feet off their pedals and whizzed down the hill towards town, Demelza's anorak cape flapping as the cold breeze pinched her nose and ears. Nessa grinned at her as they skidded around the bend at the bottom of the hill and wheelied over a little wooden bridge.

'You realize we're actual Penfurzy knights now?'

Demelza laughed. 'Wow. We are! But it's not like anyone will ever know.'

'We know,' said Nessa, 'and that's enough.'

She reached out her fist. Demelza bumped her knuckles and they rolled into town together, spit sisters, friends, Penfurzy knights, on an important quest for a nice warm scarf.

THE

END

(FOR NOW)

Acknowledgements

Oh hi, you're still here? HIGH FIVE! This is the part where I thank everyone who helped with these books and get all emotional while I write, I'll try my hardest not to drip snot onto the page. Here goes!

To Rex and Moo at Foam Sword Games, the makers of the Knights and Bikes game which the books are based on. Thanks, guys, for letting me play with your world and characters, I had so much fun, especially in Piskie Parc! Did you see all that awesome art inside this book? That's by Luke Newell. I sometimes think Luke has a little window that lets him look into my head and see exactly how I imagine the story. This is both very cool and totally terrifying.

Thank you to my wonderful agent, Hannah Shepperd, and my super-cool publishers, Knights Of – Aimée, Marssaié for her design skills and Daphne for shouting about books, and David Stevens for his trust in me, his ace editing skills and geek chat. To Sue Cook for her excellent, funny notes and insightful comments, and Steve Morton for his eagle eyes.

Big thanks to Frances, Louise, CJ, Robert, Graeme, Sarah, Julie and all of the reps working tirelessly to sell Penfurzy timeshare caravans across the UK. To Clementine and Alice for being such passionate advocates, and to Emma, Bethan and Annabelle at EDPR. So many wonderful booksellers have supported Knights and Bikes, Jenna at The Book Corner

Shop, Drake: The Bookshop, Forum Books, Waterstones Middlesbrough, Darlington, Yarm, Stockton and Northallerton and Blackwells. A special shout out to bookseller extraordinaire, Fiona Sharp at Waterstones Durham. And in Ireland, thank you to everyone at Easons, Dubray and The Gutter Bookshop for such huge support.

Squeezy hugs to all the teachers and librarians, too many to mention, who have brought Knights and Bikes to young readers. Thanks to my supportive writery friends, Sophie, Liz, Chris and my twitter friends, to Rick O'Shea, and to brilliant organisations:: Seven Stories, Booktrust, CLPE, CBI, Norwich Games Fest, Liverpool Children's Festival of Reading, Birmingham Impact Hub, Northern Children's Book Festival, National Literary Trust, Mountains To Sea and the Edinburgh Book Festival.

While editing this book I left my day job to focus on writing and on my amazing, crazy daughter, Ashoka. My family and friends were a huge help to me in this big decision, my forever supportive husband, Satish, my sister from another mister, Rhianna, my parents, brothers and wonderful in-laws, your love and cheerleading is forever appreciated.

To anyone I've missed, thank you! So many people are involved in getting a book from my brain to you, the fantabulous reader who has adventured your way through Penfurzy with Nessa, Demelza, Captain Honkers and the pickled knight. Thank you for joining us on this adventure. I hope you come back to Penfurzy soon.

ME AND NESSA HOPE YOU ENJOYED OUR ADVENTURE WHAT GABRIELLE WROTE DOWN IN THIS **BOOK!!**

YOU CAN EVEN USE MY GAME-GAUNTLET AND IT'S MAGICKAL POWERS!!

AND YOU CAN PLAY IT ON YOUR OWN, BUT ITS EVEN BETTER WITH A FRIEND!

ON PLAYSTATION 4 AND ON PC AND MAC

OR SEARCH FOR 'KNIGHTS AND BIKES' ON YOUTUBE.

WWW.FOAMSWORDGAMES.COM

GABRIELLE KENT

Gabrielle is from the North East of England. She grew up in the 1980's riding her bike into trouble, drawing monsters, reading comics and playing games on her best friend's Atari. Her first job was in video-games working on games for PC, Playstation and XBox. She taught game design to university students for sixteen years and is now a full time writer. She is the author of the Alfie Bloom series and is excited to be writing books about Nessa and Demelza, stars of the super cool video-game, Knights and Bikes.

DON'T MISS THE FIRST GREAT ADVENTURE IN

AIR
LOCK

Chapter One
WELCOME TO PENFURZY

The wind howled around the cabin like a rabid beast as the rain crashed against the windows. The occupants huddled together in terror as a shadowy figure loomed at the window, moonlight glinting off the blade in its gnarled hand...

'HONNNK!'

Demelza's torch and the comic she was reading were torn from her hands as her pet goose flapped his wings furiously, causing their blanket tent to collapse around them on the bed.

‘What is it, Captain Honkers?’ whispered Demelza, grabbing the goose and hugging him so close that his feathery cheek was squished up against her pale freckled face. ‘Are we in danger?’

She popped her head up from the crumpled pile of blankets and peered around the little caravan where they lived. Outside, the wind howled around the caravan like a rabid beast as the rain crashed against the windows. Demelza and Captain Honkers huddled together in terror as a shadowy figure loomed at the window...

Demelza let out a little squeak and dived back under the blankets as the shadow slithered towards the door. ‘Shh, Honkers!’ she hissed, shining her torch at the goose and clamping his beak shut between her thumb and forefinger before he could honk again. She peeked out from under the blanket. Whatever was out there had reached the door.

The handle rattled.

Demelza breathed a small sigh as she remembered locking the door before going to bed. Her relief was short-lived as a metallic scratching sound came from the lock.

‘It’s trying to break in!’ she squeaked at Captain Honkers.

The goose flapped his wings angrily, bursting to honk.

The lock clicked again.

Demelza took a deep breath. 'If we're going to be eaten by a carnivorous beast with three mouths and... and tentacles for arms, then we're going to go down fighting. Aren't we, Honkers?'

She snatched up a blanket, grabbed her foam sword from under her wooden bed and hid behind the door. Holding up two corners of the blanket, Demelza peered over the top and watched as the door finally creaked open.

The monster slipped inside.

'Yaaaaargh!' screamed Demelza, throwing the blanket up and over the beast.

'Honnnk!' squawked Captain Honkers, pecking furiously at the thrashing creature under the blanket.

Demelza began to whack at what she thought was its head. 'Die, creature of the night!' she yelled as the foam sword flailed. 'Begone! Back to the pit from whence you came!'

'Mkay! Kay! Ry smurunder,' burbled the creature.

Demelza stopped whacking. 'Did you hear that, Honkers?' she said, wide-eyed. 'It's trying to communicate.' She pointed her torch at the struggling blanket and prodded it with her sword. 'What did you say, foul beast?'

The creature wriggled away from her and struggled to its feet before flinging off the blanket and putting its hands up in the air. A large duffel bag containing something big and rectangular fell to the floor.

'I said, OK, I surrender!' said the demon, which Demelza had to admit was starting to look much less like hell-spawn, and more like a girl not much older than her.

She had brown skin and punky black hair. Her leather gloves were fingerless and she was wearing slouchy leather ankle boots and not one but TWO earrings in one ear. She was the coolest-looking burglar Demelza had ever seen. She was also the *first* burglar Demelza had ever seen.

The girl bent down to pick up her duffel bag and Demelza pointed her battered sword warily at her.

'You're not from here,' she said, narrowing her eyes. 'I know everyone on Penfurzy Island, and you're not anyone I know.'

'Just passing through,' said the girl, brushing the tip of the sword away, then rolling up her sleeve to rub at the little red peck marks Captain Honkers had left on her arm. 'I thought this place was empty. I'm not sticking around – I was just after somewhere to sleep tonight. Sorry I scared you. I'll be off now, OK?'

'Scared?' said Demelza, her frizzy red bunches bouncing as she leapt to block the girl's path to the door. 'We weren't scared, was we, Honkers?' She grabbed the goose and held him under one arm.

'Honk!' said Captain Honkers.

'Sure. OK, kid, you weren't scared. Now, if you'll move, I'll go and find somewhere else for the night.'

Demelza stood firm. 'Who you calling kid? What are you? Ten or eleven? You's just a kid too. So, shut up, stupid-head!'

'Say it, don't spray it,' said the girl, wiping her face with the back of her hand in an exaggerated motion.

'So, are you going to get out of my way? Or are you going to try to stab me to death with your toy sword?'

Demelza scratched her chin, accidentally picking the top off a scab she had forgotten was there. 'I haven't decided yet,' she said. 'If I do let you out, where'll you go?'

The girl shrugged as she slung her bag over her shoulder. 'What's it to you, short stuff?'

The wind whistled around the caravan, blowing open the door and driving the icy rain forcefully against the windows. Demelza could see goose pimples all over the girl's arms. Her hair and jeans were also dripping wet and she was only wearing a T-shirt under her light denim jacket.

Demelza chewed her lip. Even though this very strange stranger had invaded their fortress, suggested that she was scared, AND called her short, she wouldn't send even her worst enemy out near the cliffs on a stormy night like this. It was a night just like this when her own mother had—

Demelza shivered and made a decision. She slammed the flapping door shut, locked it and pretended to swallow the key. 'You're not going nowhere. Not tonight,' she said firmly, then picked up her blanket and held it out to the girl. 'Honkers sez you can stay here with me an' him. He can sleep in my bed with me, and you can use the top bunk.'

The girl pushed her wet hair out of her eyes and shrugged as though she'd be just as happy going back out in the rain, but Demelza could see a look of relief under the façade.

'Yeah, I guess I could chill here for a few hours,' the girl said. 'Long as you keep that Honkers on your side of the room in case he tries to murder me in the middle of the night.'

'That's *Captain* Honkers to you,' said Demelza, putting the goose down on her bed and wrapping him up in a blanket. 'He only lets *me* call him Honkers.'

She finished tucking the goose in, kissed him on the top of his head and turned to give the girl a sharp stare.

'Besides, as far as we know, *you* could be the type that does murdering – sneaking around at night, breaking into people's bedrooms. The only way to know that you won't do a murder on us in our sleep is if we're friends.' She wiped her hand on her faded pyjama bottoms and held it out. 'You've got to know someone's name if you're going to be friends. I'm Demelza. Demelza Penrose. I'm nine and five months. I like comics, drawing, riding my bike and playing computer games. My favourite food is banana and peanut butter sandwiches, and I have a scar on my right knee from when Connan Lenteglos, the most annoying boy at school, dared me to do a one hundred and eighty bunny hop on my bike. I totally did it, though!' she said proudly. 'Right. Now it's your turn.'

The girl paused for a minute, looking at Demelza's outstretched hand. Demelza wiggled her fingers and gave her biggest and friendliest grin, the one that showed all her teeth.

The girl finally took Demelza's hand with half a smile. 'I'm Nessa,' she said.

'Just... Nessa?' said Demelza. 'One name, that's it?'

'Yeah. You know, like Prince.'

Demelza screwed up her forehead. 'Prince who?'

'It doesn't matter,' grinned Nessa, making Demelza feel she was missing out on a joke.

'Well then. Pleased to meet you, O mysterious Nessa,' said Demelza, shaking her hand firmly. 'The captain and I officially welcome you to Penfurzy, the bestest island in the whole wide world!'

'Honk!' said Captain Honkers.

'You're right, Honkers. She does look hungry. Nessa, we shall throw a feast in your honour!'

READ WHAT HAPPENS NEXT IN

KNIGHTS AND BIKES

AVAILABLE IN BOOKSHOPS NOW!

CAN'T WAIT FOR THE NEXT

KNIGHTS AND BIKES

by Gabrielle Kent

CHECK OUT OTHER BOOKS FROM **KNIGHTS OF**:

HIGH-RISE MYSTERY?

GHOST

by **JASON REYNOLDS**

AVAILABLE IN BOOKSHOPS NOW